The Cowboy's
Mail-Order Bride

The Cowboy's Mail-Order Bride

A Careys of Cowboy Point Novel

Megan Crane

TULE
PUBLISHING

Dedication

To Jane, for everything, as always.

Prologue

ZEKE CAREY CONSIDERED himself a damned lucky man.

Maybe the luckiest man alive, though he didn't like to brag. He liked the facts of his life to do the bragging for him. His father had always said that there was no need for boasting if a man's life was well-lived.

Zeke had taken that to heart.

He'd been fortunate enough to be born in the finest part of the Rocky Mountains in the last, best place around—that being the great and glorious state of Montana. The only state in the Union he had ever or would ever live in, God willing, and that he'd never had to test that theory was a blessing he had never taken for granted. Not for a single day in his many long years of working the land.

Because the land was the thing.

The land was what woke him in the morning, kept him going, and what he dreamed about at night. Zeke was the current steward of the land his ancestors had claimed high above Paradise Valley, a job and a calling he had taken seriously since he was a kid.

Since he'd worked with his grandfather and his uncles and his own father, tending to these acres like they were all marked indelibly inside his own heart.

He planned to go out the way a man of the land should, right here, surrounded by these rolling hills and then a part of them.

Though, hopefully, not any time soon.

These days, though, something was changing, and it wasn't the expected indignities of age and time. Or not *only* said indignities.

Truth was, he was lucky enough to know that age and time were the greatest gifts of all.

Still, these days Zeke found himself waking in the morning with other kinds of legacies on his mind.

He started his days the same way each morning. He woke in the dark long before his wife, and set about the calming rituals—he called them *routines*, mind—that saw in each new stretch of daylight, however little they were getting of it in the darker, colder months. First he made sure the stove that heated the house was stoked a little hotter and higher, because it might have been spring in a technical sense, but up here in the mountains that didn't mean it was any less cold.

When Zeke peered outside, he saw fresh snow.

It was late March. Sometimes they saw snow straight through June.

In the kitchen of the rambling old ranch house, he ground up some beans and made the coffee extra strong, anticipating his wife's complaints about the weather. Complaints she made, without fail, each and every day—her own kind of love song to this place.

Love, Zeke knew, was a complicated thing.

He should know, having had the great fortune to know two great loves in his life, as well as the deep grief that was the other side of it when he'd buried the first.

Alice had been like a soft, warm spring rain. Her love had made him feel clean. He wasn't the only thing that had bloomed in the shine of her rare smile.

He'd started thinking that life was about earning those smiles when he was fourteen, and had continued that practice until Alice's last breath.

Belinda, by contrast, was a storm. Thunder, lightning, howling wind—but the end result was the same. She washed away the bad and accepted only the good.

He was a lucky man to have loved twice, so well and so deeply.

Maybe that was why he was thinking less about the land these days, and more about legacies of blood and bone.

Alice had given him three sons, Belinda two.

They were all impossible, just like their father.

Zeke eyed the parade of photographs that dominated the hall as he walked down it, then into the sunniest room of the house. Even on a chilly day like today, with March gloom threatening, the little room seemed cozy.

It was here that he and Alice had hidden away when the babies were asleep at last. Where they had sat together and told each other stories about the future they didn't know, then, wasn't theirs to plan. It was here that he had kissed her forehead for the last time and told her to go, that it was okay to leave.

And it was here, again, that he had asked Belinda to marry him. And where she had given birth to each of their sons together.

This room was made entirely of love. It was his favorite room in the house.

He settled into his usual chair, tipping his cup toward the large photograph that always sat there on the table beside him, facing out toward the sweeping view. The best damned view in Montana, to his mind, and that was a high bar.

Alice had always loved this particular view from this particular place. That was why Belinda had insisted that Zeke's favorite picture of her stay right here with them, because while she would have stayed longer if she could have, that she'd gone was why Zeke and Belinda were together.

He had been happy with Alice. He would have stormed heaven to give her more time.

It had never occurred to him that he could be happy again, but he was. He was luckier than he deserved and he knew it.

These days, it was his five hard-headed sons who didn't seem to understand that life was fleeting and nothing was promised but here. Now.

More to the point, Zeke was getting tired of his own

sons—that he'd made out of two great love stories, not that they seemed to know it—depriving him of what a man of his advancing years wanted most.

Grandchildren.

Delightful small humans he didn't have to worry about turning into decent men, so could spoil at will.

"You have that look on your face," Belinda said, coming into the room and stopping beside him. She nodded at the photograph of Alice. "You know," she said, addressing the photograph the way she always did, making it clear that Alice was here with both of them, not just Zeke. That she always would be. He would have loved her for that alone. "The last time you looked like that we ended up with alpacas in the back pasture."

Belinda settled on the arm of the chair and leaned against his shoulder, and they fit together the way they always did. Better by the year. Zeke loved these slow mornings, now that the boys—because they would always be his boys, though they were inarguably grown now—were out of the house. If there was sunlight, it poured in. Today they could see almost all the way to Copper Mountain, rising in the distance.

They took their coffee here. They talked to Alice. They teased each other. They worried and laughed about the funny little children who were *men* now.

Sometimes they found themselves naked on the floor together, because it had always been like that with them, a passion that could not contain itself.

A storm, Zeke thought. Always a storm.

They lived everywhere else. They did their work, they handled their business and their days.

This room was for breathing in and taking a moment. For the simple joy of being together.

"Folks like wool," Zeke told Alice gruffly, sending Belinda into gales of laughter.

"Not enough to justify more creatures to feed and care for every day," she replied, after wiping at her eyes. "And besides, I'm not one of those folks who like wool."

The alpacas had not been a hit. Zeke had sold them off to a far more alpaca-friendly outfit, who were in fact wool lovers and sold knitted goods and skeins of hand-dyed yarn in the weekly summer market.

Not all great ideas became legacies. He knew that.

But he was having a truly fantastic idea all the same.

"What would you say if I decided to be... a little bit devious?" Zeke asked, his mind turning as he stared out at the land and the hills, and the hints of smoke here and there from the chimneys in the cabins their sons lived in. Alone.

"What I always say." His wife smiled at him, angelically. "Lie to me and I will gut you, my one and only love."

"So bloodthirsty." He kissed her. Then he pulled her into his lap. "You and I are going to have to take matters into our own hands if we want the life we deserve. The grandparent life," he qualified when she frowned at him. "Sometimes a parent has to allow a child to think something that's not strictly true. For that child's own good."

"Zeke," Belinda said piously, "I cannot allow you to lie to our beloved children. What do you take me for?" But she grinned. "Unless we have to. And in this case, we clearly have no choice. They are too slow."

"No choice at all," Zeke agreed solemnly as she wrapped her arms around his neck.

"I'm sure it will hurt us more than it hurts them," Belinda murmured.

And then they laughed and laughed as he told her what he planned to do.

For their own good.

Chapter One

HARLAN CAREY KNEW the woman who rushed in through the doors of Grey's Saloon and then stopped dead, as if she needed to do a quick reconnaissance of the place before she could commit to it, was his very own mail-order bride.

They got their fair share of tourists here in Marietta, a small town tucked away in Paradise Valley, Montana, where folks liked to stop before heading down to explore the many glories of Yellowstone and the Grand Tetons. But he knew she wasn't headed out to explore any national parks in this stretch of May that was called spring but was still too cold to mean it.

He knew she was here for him.

Harlan knew this instantly and without question, the way his late mother used to say she knew things she shouldn't—down deep in the bones. The way the weather was going to turn up on Copper Mountain. The way the sun settled down into the hills in winter, just a gleam of gold to remind a man hunkering down in the Montana cold that the light always came back eventually. The way he could eyeball a fractious calf before it got itself in too much trouble and more often than not, sort out the situation before it developed. The way he had that sixth sense about when his fences—or his family—needed his attention.

It was her.

Though if he was right about that, and he knew he was, it was going to be a problem.

Harlan knew that just as certainly and just as quick.

She'd come in with the wind when she'd opened the door and Harlan could feel the bite of it on the back of his neck. He'd driven down the side of Copper Mountain this morning, still snowy and icy most of the way to the valley floor. It was that snow and ice you could feel even walking around the streets of Marietta, a reminder that seasons in Montana were more like suggestions. Folks liked to claim there were only three: winter, July, and August.

Sure, there were hints of spring if a man knew where to look, but it was different in the higher elevations, where Harlan had lived all his life. High Mountain Ranch had been in his family since his rugged, determined ancestors had made the trek out from various forms of indentured servitude in the East to try their hand at mining. Copper Mountain hadn't turned out to have a lot of copper, despite grand promises to the contrary. The Careys, always quick to pivot when necessary, had decided to claim as much land as they could—far away enough from the bustle of town and the copper and railway barons who thought too highly of themselves in their fancy Victorian houses.

That was how High Mountain Ranch had been born. Grit, determination, a kind of steel-plated optimism, and more than a little bullheadedness.

Harlan's great-grandfather, the wily and much-mustachioed Matthew Carey, had been a terrible miner by all accounts, but had turned out to have a way with the land. Harlan liked to think that way of his had been passed down through the years, eldest son to eldest son and sometimes the rest of the family too.

Today it sat on him hard, the duty that went with a legacy like that. Not the land, because land was a terrible gift and a beautiful struggle, and a man could spend a lifetime navigating a course between the two. But that part was easy, ultimately, because what the land took it also gave back, in its way.

It was things like what he was doing today that hit harder. Things that were about the land, but felt more personal than that, because duty had sharp teeth.

He was sitting in Grey's Saloon in pretty little Marietta, which was technically the town he lived in. Only technically, though, because the community Matthew Carey and other likeminded ex-miners and prospectors had settled into was ten miles up Copper Mountain, around on the backside where folks liked to say they were caught between the Lord and the lunatics.

They'd dubbed the area Cowboy Point and like many places around here, there was some debate as to how Cowboy Point had come by its name. Some claimed it had been a joke. That the miners, known for a certain level of gallows humor necessary to surviving their profession, had called it that because there weren't any cowboys. Not at first. These days Harlan supposed the name fit better. There were real cowboys, like him. Then again, some would argue that anyone who lived out here in the Montana backcountry, far away from the ritzy comforts of Bozeman or Jackson Hole, was a cowboy where it counted.

Though Harlan thought he'd never done anything that was quite so much the old-school cowboy way as this: Putting an ad in the paper for a proper wife like it was still the 1850s.

He'd regretted almost the moment he'd done it, but by then it had been too late.

And now, here he was. Sitting at a table watching a woman scan the place, looking for him. Looking for the kind of man he wished he wasn't—that being the kind of man who needed to put an ad out for a woman in the first place.

It all sat different, now, this game he'd decided to play and then decided to pretend he hadn't bothered with. And he knew it was because of her.

She wasn't what he wanted at all.

He watched her pivot, her gaze sweeping over the weathered old saloon that gleamed this early in the day. Behind the bar, the longtime owner Jason Gray stood with his usual military precision, seemingly unaware of anything around him while he looked down at a stack of papers. But anyone local, or observant, knew that very little got past the old Marine.

Harlan knew that Jason was fully aware that this woman was looking around like she was casing the joint. There was something about the way her eyes narrowed. Something about the way she paused a little on each thing she saw before moving onto the next, like she was memorizing it. The long stretch of polished bar itself. The pool table in the back. The jukebox that Jason stubbornly refused to update to reflect modern music no matter how many times he was asked. It seemed to take her a long time to get back around to the set of booths along the far wall, then travel to the one way back in the corner where Harlan sat.

There was one other table in here. A local family Harlan knew enough to nod to on the way in, but not enough to stop and talk much. But that was a good thing, because it meant they might not pay too much attention to him, either.

He kept his eyes trained on the woman. The woman who was here to see if she'd like to become his wife, something that seemed a little more intense and real now than it had while he'd been driving down the mountain earlier, wondering what the hell he was doing.

In his truck, it had seemed like a game. But not any longer.

Her gaze locked with his and he thought, *at last*.

That settled in him strangely, but he ignored it. He nodded a greeting, reaching up to tip down his Stetson in front. And then whatever was taking its time settling in his gut took even longer, because she reacted to that. To the tip of his hat.

Like it hit her the same way her gaze had hit him.

She seemed to come close to swaying on her feet, which was more intriguing than he wanted to let on, even to himself. Maybe especially to himself. Then she started toward him anyway.

As she walked in his direction, Harlan stood up from the booth because he had been raised to show respect to a woman that way. And also because he wanted to see just how high on his chest the top of her head would hit.

Which, neatly enough, laid out the whole problem with her that he could see from across the room. The problem he'd seen the moment she'd walked in.

She was pretty.

Inarguably pretty, in all the ways he liked.

It was a complication Harlan had not been expecting.

Though his body was not exactly processing it as a *complication*.

She took her time walking across the nearly empty saloon to his booth and he learned a lot about her, watching her move. Her eyes were narrow as she looked back at him with more than a little suspicion. She lifted her chin in a way that either showed she was confident or belligerent. Hard to say which. And she let her gaze travel over him, taking in his usual jeans and boots and the button-down shirt he had worn for the occasion.

He reckoned that meant he could do the same in return, so he did. Her hair looked glossy and silky, caught back in a high ponytail that moved when she did. It was the color of deep, rich earth shot through with sunlight. Her eyes looked greener the closer she came. She had a clever, angular face—a contrast to her full mouth and he had the sense she knew it. That there was a little extra color on her lips to play that up, that contrast.

She was lean all over, bordering on skinny but packed into a pair of jeans that did mouthwatering things to her butt and her long legs, then ended up in a pair of motorcycle boots that look scuffed and worn—but not like they'd ever been near a motorcycle in their lifetime. She wore a formfitting tank top that peeked out from underneath a looser buttoned shirt, yet none of that managed to give her much bulk. She had the kind of hip bones that were obvious to the naked eye, immediately making him a little too interested wrapping his hands around them while he rolled her beneath—

There it was again. The reason why this was a terrible idea. And why he was going to have to say hello to her and then send her on her way. Maybe he'd buy her lunch for her trouble, but she was a walking quagmire and Harlan didn't have time for quicksand of any description.

He was carrying too much as it was.

She came to a stop before him. Her hands found her hips and for a moment they stood there, each finishing up their little survey of the other.

Turned out that the top of her head came to just above the center of his chest.

The perfect height, by his estimation.

For the record.

"I take it you're Harlan Carey," she said, with a hint of the South in her voice. Tennessee, if he had to guess. That mouth of hers twitched a little and it took effort not to watch that twitch too closely. "Or I expect I've been stood up."

"That would make you Kendall Darlington," he drawled.

He tipped his hat again and then waved a hand toward the booth, inviting her to sit. Then watched her... hesitate.

It was only the faintest hesitation, but Harlan realized he was... not used to that.

Women did not usually *hesitate* around him. He might not have his brothers' well-earned reputation for mixing it up and for always being available for one kind of party or another, but that had never stopped the right kind of cowgirl.

And it had been a long while—or maybe it had never happened, because he was Harlan Carey and his stalwart, upstanding reputation always did the talking for him—that he'd watched a woman try to work out if she should trust him.

Here, now, under these admittedly strange circumstances, it felt like a victory and a relief when she did.

She slid across the bench seat so she could put her back to the wall and face him on a diagonal. And there were the makings of a smile on her face, or the promise of one, but her gaze was moving around the saloon again. Like she was looking for something.

Or waiting for something, maybe.

"You on the run?" he asked.

And he was kidding, mostly, until something moved over her face. Almost as if he'd startled her—but then it was gone so fast that he couldn't be entirely sure he'd seen anything at all.

"I like to see what's coming," she replied, and smiled like that was a joke.

Though he didn't think it was.

Harlan settled in the booth across from her, and he hadn't really thought about this part. The fact that there would be conversation to make and he was going to have to make it. It wasn't that he couldn't do it. His brother Wilder liked to claim that Harlan preferred cattle to humans. Wilder's twin, Ryder, always said Harlan was having a love affair with the mountains and had no room for people. The youngest two Carey brothers, Boone and Knox, usually contented themselves with eye rolls.

Harlan had never been one for small talk, that was true enough. He was a Montanan. He was genetically indisposed to *small* of any kind. But he reminded himself, then, that this wasn't a date. She'd answered an ad. She'd been interested enough in his terse few sentences about what he was looking for to reply.

All he had to do was try not to be less appealing than that ad.

That was when he remembered that what he actually needed to do here was send her on her way so he could get back to the business of finding himself a wife who fit his requirements. Who wasn't this... distracting.

"So," Kendall said when all he could manage was to frown at her a little. "I expected you to be... older." When he blinked, not sure how to take that, she laughed. And it was a real laugh, he could tell. It made her nose scrunch up, and something inside him did, too. "You don't look like the kind of person who has to put an ad out to find himself a wife, that's all."

"But you're the sort of person who answers an ad like that?" he asked, since they were getting it right out in the open. "Thinking it would be some old geezer? Not to draw any conclusions about the kind of woman who would be into that sort of thing."

She tilted her head to the side, as if deciding against a set of responses, which only made him want to know what she *almost* said. "I was expecting some sort of visible explanation to help me figure out why a man would actually place an ad like that." She laughed again, and it was a lighter sound, but there was no scrunching of her nose this time. "It's so old-fashioned I naturally assumed you must be, too."

"I have my moments," Harlan replied, because that laugh might have been fake but she was *gazing* at him.

He really hadn't banked on her being pretty. That hadn't been in the plans at all. He was still trying to get his bearings in the face of it.

"Are you a serial killer?" she asked him, in the same light, airy tone.

Disarming him, he suspected. On purpose.

"No ma'am," he replied, and that easily, he felt significantly more comfortable. He found himself drawling. And he was awfully close to enjoying himself, suddenly—though on him that turned into stern. "What I am is boring. I wake up before the sun. I eat, sleep, and dream about the land. I'm a rancher, bones and blood and everything in between. It's not what I do, it's who I am."

She seemed to consider that carefully. "Why do you want a wife?"

He threaded his fingers together there on the table, between them. "My father is a stubborn man." That was an understatement when it came to the legendary Zeke Carey, but there was no point poisoning the well straight out of the gate. If she stuck around and wanted to drink from that well, the good news was that it was always going to be there. In one form or another. "A force of nature all his life. Until last month at Easter dinner with all of my brothers home and sitting around the table, he made an announcement."

"I don't know what question to ask first." She looked as if she was testing those questions internally and, once again, he wanted to know the ones she didn't feel she could ask. "How many brothers do you have? And do you really all gather for Easter dinner?"

She said *Easter dinner* like he'd confessed that he was from a family of mimes who performed instead of eating, but he just filed that away until there was time to analyze it all. Until he had some distance from the prettiness, those clever eyes, that *mouth*.

Until he could think straight himself. Not an issue he'd ever grappled with before.

"I have four brothers," he said. "And yes, we do Easter dinner. We also do a Sunday dinner every week. My brother Ryder isn't always home so when he is, it's extra special. This one was even more special because our dad told us that that he's taken poorly."

Harlan didn't like to think about it. It had been a whole month already and it still felt… impossible. But that was something else he didn't intend to get into with a stranger who didn't even know that Zeke Carey was like the whole, big Montana sky. That it was *impossible* to imagine life without him.

He didn't *want* to imagine it, so he kept talking, getting the toughest part out as quick as he could. "He told us there was no cure. We have about a year." Harlan blew out a breath. "And in that time, he'd like to see all five of us married because he has a hankering for some grandchildren. Might not get to meet them, but he'd sure like to know they're on the way before he's gone."

She sat with that for a moment, like she could see how hard that was for him to say at all, much less so matter-of-factly.

"I'm sorry," she said after a breath or two. And she didn't do what some folks did, getting intense and flowery because they didn't know what to say. Not Kendall. She let it sit there, as stark as the reality that no one in Harlan's family wanted to face.

Hell, as far as Harlan knew, not a one of his brothers had even accepted it. Much less acted upon Zeke's instructions.

"I appreciate that," he said, and he did. But Harlan didn't want to dwell on it. "My brothers all have better social lives than I do, likely because they work less than I do." He knew that wasn't fair, but none of his brothers were here to protest. So, too bad. "I knew that if I wanted to honor the old man's wishes I was going to have to take action."

"A very Old West sort of action."

"Here's the thing, Kendall." And he really focused on her, then. On the wary way she was sitting. At that suspicious look in her eyes. At the line of her throat and how it found her collarbone in a way that a man was likely to find entirely too distracting, if he gave it any thought. "I spend all my time on the land. When I'm not out handling the stock and the chores, there's paperwork. My dad has slowed down a lot in recent years, so I picked up the slack. That's not a complaint, it's just a fact."

"Noted."

"I don't have time to date." He had said that a lot, over the years. But it felt different saying it to her, the woman he wasn't dating who had come here to talk marriage all the same. "I need a woman who's practical, down-to-earth, and prepared to be a partner in the work we do. A woman who's willing to get her hands dirty on day one. I'm not sure dinner and a drink is going to lead to any of that. Not in a timely fashion. And time is one thing I don't have."

"Your ad was very direct and to the point."

And he couldn't tell if that gleam in her green gaze was laughter, possibly even a bit of mockery. But if it was the latter, it was the kind that felt more like fingernails dancing down the length of his back than scraping down a chalkboard.

He wasn't sure it did him any good to note the difference.

Kendall reached into her back pocket and pulled out a mobile phone, swiping until she opened her pictures. She tilted the phone to show him the screen, and he recognized it at once. It was a picture of the ad he'd put out, in the personal section of a whole slew of regional newspapers, online and off.

Cowboy looking for wife to work the land, help with the

business, and raise the next generation. Must be practical, reasonable, and honest.

"I can't decide," she said, in a musing sort of tone, "if I think you got a thousand replies or none."

"You replied," he pointed out.

"How many of these interviews have you had?"

He didn't like the word *interview*, or the way she'd said it. He figured that was on purpose, because it turned out that Kendall Darlington was a little spiky. But a Montanan had to have a little spice to go along with the grit or none of them would survive the dark months, and summer was a beautiful thing but life here was the dark months. There were a whole lot more of them.

"You're the one and only," he told her. "Everyone else who asked for one… wasn't right."

He could have told her about the people who'd offered to send him nudes. About the ones who went ahead and did just that. About the people who'd sent abuse, religious tracts concerning the state of his soul, and lectures about how he should meet a nice girl at home. He could have told her about those who had written him long, involved sob stories about their disastrous lives like marrying him—or anyone—could change that.

There was the widow from Winnemucca who'd assured him that God had put it on her heart that he was, in fact, her husband. He hadn't responded, figuring God could take care of the miscommunication if He wanted. There had been the unhinged woman who'd told him she was moving to Montana anyway and wouldn't it be a coincidence she ended up near him, so maybe they should marry right off the bat? He hadn't responded to her either, though he did keep an eye out when he drove down into town.

He had only responded to this one.

I'm not afraid of work or cowboys, she'd replied. *And I'm prepared to be as practical, reasonable, and honest as you are, if that works.*

In his head, the woman he'd imagined would write that kind of response had been… different. He'd figured she'd be older too, though he wasn't going to say that. He'd imagined a plain, hardy woman. A woman who might not get a second look from most, but who would distinguish herself in other ways. Her steadfastness, true and real, over time.

Like his own mother, Alice, who they'd lost when Harlan was eight. She hadn't been a raving beauty by any objective standard. The photographs made that clear and he'd never seen any evidence that she'd tried to change that in the way some women did. But there'd always been a glow about her. Anyone who looked at her looked back, then looked longer. Everyone who'd ever met her loved her. She'd been sturdy and even-tempered and she'd made everything better with her brand of quiet, stubborn competence.

He'd envisioned a woman like that.

Not Kendall, whose angles looked sharp and made him think about all the sorts of edges he could play with—

"Meeting you," Kendall was saying with a shrug, "I have to say that you're not what I was expecting at all."

"Not old enough. Or weird enough. Those sound like good things."

She didn't deny that. "I understand all your reasons, but you still don't strike me as the kind of man who would resort to an ad no matter what your reasons are. It doesn't seem to go hand in hand with a full-on Stetson and the Cowboy Code outfit you have down to the shiny belt buckle." Before he could respond to that, she tilted her head to the side again. "I bet that that red truck outside is yours, too. That vintage pickup that I bet you don't use for photo shoots."

"It was my grandfather's. I use it for the same things he did. Ranch work." He resisted the urge to reach across the table. He didn't even know where it came from. "It wasn't my idea to run an ad. I was pretty sure it was a spectacularly bad idea the minute I did it, but here you are. And that begs a question all its own, doesn't it?"

Kendall leaned in closer to the table, and propped her chin up on her hand. "Does it?"

It did. And suddenly there wasn't a thing Harlan wanted more in the world than her answer. "You're very pretty, Kendall."

Some women would blush at that. Or get flustered and try to pretend otherwise.

Kendall only gazed back at him, her gaze green and unreadable. "That wasn't a question."

"Try this." Harlan leaned in a little himself and took pleasure in the way her breath caught. "Why would a pretty girl like you answer an ad like mine at all, much less come all this way to meet me—sight unseen—when there was such a high probability I'd be that weird old guy you expected?"

Chapter Two

THIS WAS A mistake.

Kendall Darlington knew it. She'd suspected it before she'd come down to Marietta today—because who was she kidding, thinking she could escape her family that easily—and she'd known it for sure the minute she'd walked into this old timey saloon that looked like it belonged in a movie. Something involving high noon shoot-outs and men with gravelly drawls who loved their horses more than their women.

A classic country song, basically.

She'd instantly decided to leave and yet here she was anyway. Sitting at a table, a little too close to flirting with this man for comfort.

When she'd decided to do this thing, she'd accepted that she would have to flirt a little bit. Maybe more than *a little bit*, if necessary. Because if her mother had ever taught her anything, and that was by no means certain, it was the magical properties of *just* the right amount of flirting.

Men love to feel like men, her mother would say with a mouth full of the South mixed with vodka on ice. *The best thing a girl can do is let him.*

Kendall tried to shake that off, because she knew too well that no good came of dwelling too much on the quotable things Mayrose Darlington said. Because Mayrose was... a lot of things. Too many things, some might say, and Kendall usually did.

Quotable was perhaps the most lovable of them.

What Mayrose was currently, Kendall needed to remember, was not *here*. That was the critical bit.

Kendall had packed up and left in the middle of the night, and had known better than to leave behind even a hint of where she might be going. The last time she'd done that had been her attempt to emancipate herself from the curse of the Darlingtons when she'd been all of eighteen, and that had ended badly on a side street in Cranston, Rhode Island. Operatic scenes and recriminations and no escape, after all.

This time she'd slipped away quietly. She'd taken a bus from Coeur d'Alene, Idaho, all the way to Livingston, Montana, because Darlingtons were not bus people and she knew they wouldn't think to look at bus schedules.

Even if they did, why would they look off in the middle of Montana?

She'd spent a couple of nights in Livingston, at the top of what they called Paradise Valley, wandering around the old western cattleman's city with its neon saloon lights and insistent, demanding wind—the kind of wind that cut through a body so hard it made her want to let it blow her back across the Great Plains to Chicago.

It was the kind of wind that made her think she ought to consider a prayer or two for deliverance. But Kendall wasn't the praying kind. What she was—what she'd been taught to be all her life—was a very particular kind of practical.

And she liked Livingston for that. There were enough tourists mixed in with the locals in the bars and restaurants to make it worth it, coming out all this way.

If necessary, she could settle down for a minute or two there, she'd thought. She could make things work the way she knew how. She could take a breath while she figured out what to do next and how best to stay as far away from her troublesome kinfolk as possible.

But first there was this Hail Mary pass of hers that she was almost entirely sure would not only fail to work, but would have her hightailing it away from Marietta and the man she'd arranged to meet here as soon as she could.

Maybe a wiser woman than she'd turned out to be would have taken that breath in Livingston and thought better of the whole thing. But Kendall was a Darlington, and Darlingtons were renowned for a certain cunning—and *cunning* wasn't the same thing as *wise*. This morning, she'd taken another bus down to Marietta, bracing herself for one of those decrepit and broke-down rural towns that looked like only the ghosts had bothered settling in for more than a season, and had been dismayed to find the place… charming.

She'd told herself—repeatedly—to ignore the charm. Or to look through it, anyway, because she knew too well that charm could often hide darker, dirtier things beneath it.

Mind you, she didn't see much that was darker or dirtier as she walked around town in the hour she'd had between checking into her hotel and when she was supposed to meet up with her potential husband-to-be. It was chillier than it looked, but then, there was still snow up in the mountains. Still, the folks she passed on the sidewalks murmured greetings as they crossed her field of vision. Men and women alike.

And they didn't seem to want anything from her in return.

While she was still a bit disoriented from all that, she'd found her way to the saloon and forced herself to see what she'd signed herself up for.

Potentially signed yourself up for, she'd reminded herself sternly as she'd gone in. *It's not like you signed a contract or made a vow.*

She'd expected him to be deeply sad, at the very least, if not old and decrepit. That was the best-case scenario. Kendall had thought it was far more likely that he might turn out to be creepy and weird, or outright scary in a worst-case scenario, and that was why she would have insisted on a public meeting place if he hadn't suggested it himself. That was also why she'd gotten herself a room at the fancy-pants hotel in town, a renovated Old West charmer called the

Graff that reminded her of the hotel she'd walked by up in Livingston. Both harkened back to the dusty, distant, cowboy past, and made her want to do things she didn't do, like belt out country songs in the street and try a little two-stepping while she was at it.

Kendall figured she could hole up in the Graff if she needed to, and this man would have to make it past the front desk, the concierge, and all the rest of that high class hotel rigmarole before he could get to her. If he turned out to be that kind of guy.

But then she'd seen Harlan.

The minute she'd walked into Grey's Saloon.

It was less that *she'd seen him* and more like she'd walked straight into a wall. The wall being *him*, sitting there in the corner the way he'd been.

Looking… like that.

Her first, wild thought was a fervent wish that he might be the man she was here to meet, because wouldn't that mean her luck was finally changing for the better?

But Kendall had been forced to become a realist a long time ago, and so she'd quickly assured herself that it was impossible. It couldn't be the man she'd arranged to meet through a series of anonymized and stiffly formal emails. Why would a man who looked like *that* be trolling for a wife in weird little papers across the West when he could just… crook a finger? She'd looked around and had assumed that if it was anyone, it was the man behind the bar, which was its own mountain to climb—but the hard look he'd thrown her way told her otherwise. It was a *don't approach me and mind yourself while you're at it* sort of look.

Kendall knew better than to mess with a man like that.

She'd still been uncertain, though she'd started over for the cowboy in the corner because he was the only possible option. And she'd been amazed and a little shocked that her body was reacting the way it was. That her heart was getting silly in her chest. She told herself it was just that she knew how her mother was going to react to this. Mayrose wouldn't take it well that Kendall had left. She and Breanna, Kendall younger sister, were likely in the middle of staging a whole, drawn-out saga about Kendall's cruel betrayal of them. Of the family. Of all they stood for, blah blah blah.

There were going to be so many scenes when they caught up with her, the way they inevitably would because they always did, that it almost crushed her then and there. It almost got her wheeling around and running back out to see if she could catch another bus right then and there to take her all the way back to that rundown hotel in Idaho where she'd left them. So she could sneak back in and pretend she hadn't meant to leave, not really. So she could smooth it all over, the way she always did, and keep everything moving along.

Because she knew she was going to end up doing it anyway.

Kendall had to give herself a talking to as she walked

across the old saloon floor, which too many cowboys to count had walked before her. It was obvious with every step. She could almost feel the weight of all that history, all those polished and battered boots, beneath her own feet.

The fact was that the life her family led was an unsustainable and unmitigated disaster. The only reason they managed to convince themselves it wasn't *that bad* was because Kendall made it not that bad. She was the peacemaker. She was the voice of reason. She was the one who had to jump in when things got too intense and find a way to talk, wheedle, or charm them back out of it.

And it had been going on so long now that she'd started to think that maybe she needed it, too, the way her sister always told her she did. That maybe she was the one who kept it all going, for some mysterious internal purpose she didn't know of yet. That was what her mother liked to claim when she was in one of her *moods of mystery* that mostly consisted of her making *dark prophecies* she pretended were another kind of family legacy.

Darlingtons were not witches. They never had been. Though they sure seemed to enjoy embodying a term that rhymed with *witches*.

Kendall knew that her family legacy was far more prosaic. They were nothing if not a whole bunch of hapless frogs sitting in a pot of hot water. And every year the heat got turned up more and more.

And she, by God, was the only one who had the sense to

jump out.

If you go back, she'd told herself as she crossed the saloon, *you're going to have to jump right into that boiling water and it's going to scald you.*

But then the cowboy who couldn't possibly be the man she was supposed to meet stood up from that booth and she felt scalded anyway.

Old and *sad* or even *scary* shouldn't be packaged like he was. He was... impossible.

The kind of man a girl was better off not dreaming about in the first place, because he could never be real.

But there he was.

He was well over six feet and every inch of him looked tough and hardpacked into those western clothes he wore. There wasn't an inch of visible fat on the man's rangy frame. It was all muscle. Lean and strong, and beneath that hat he had dirty-blond hair, intense dark eyes, and a face that looked the way she imagined statues of angels might look in all those museums her family refused to visit. Impossibly beautiful, but carved into stone.

She didn't have the slightest idea why a man like this was resorting to putting ads in a paper for a bride like it was still the Gold Rush and an ad was the only way to get a woman to come out West. In fact, Kendall was pretty sure that if this man went and stood outside the saloon on the sidewalk, he'd have an epic traffic jam of women vying for his attention even though, when she'd walked in, there had barely been a car to be seen.

"Are you going to answer me?" he asked, with a glint in those dark eyes and that *drawl* that wasn't Southern, but pure cowboy. And it… *did things* to her. "Because if you don't, I'm going to have to get a little imaginative. I guess I can't really think what would entice someone like you to answer that at all. Much less come all the way here."

"You know where I came from?" she asked, but not suspiciously. More out of interest in how he could possibly know something like that than any concern that he actually knew it.

"Ma'am," he said, and there was a grin in his voice, and on his face, if not quite on that hard, stern, fascinating mouth of his, "you're not from here. And that means that you had to work a bit to get here. I don't have to know the coordinates of where you came from to know that."

And now, the more she sat here across the table from all of that hard-edged cowboy goodness, the more Kendall realized the enormity of the mistake she'd made.

This was the trouble with the kind of life she'd led, and it didn't matter if she'd never chosen it. This is why there were sayings like, *lie down with the dogs and you get up with fleas*. She was so used to that hot pot existence that she'd just assumed that whoever this man was, she'd know how to play him.

Because everybody had a game, and the first thing she'd learned, growing up with a woman like Mayrose, was that she'd better figure out how to play whatever game was happening that day, and well.

Her whole life might depend on it. And often did.

But she didn't have to know a single thing about Harlan Carey to understand that he was not the game playing type.

He was deadly serious.

Not only that, he was honest. Kendall knew every kind of con there was. Earnestness could be a put-on, but Harlan's kind of actual honesty—written all over his face and obvious even down to the way he held himself—was the one thing a con man found hard to ape.

The vision she'd had of him—that his land was probably a farm or even a garden in the backyard, because what could *land* really mean and so she could pretend in turn, something she figured she could draw out through most of the summer if she really wanted—shimmered in her head, then disappeared.

If this man said he had land, she figured he meant what he said. And if that was true, everything he'd put in his ad might well be true, too.

And what could she legitimately say to him? *I answered your ad because I thought that I could shine you on as long as necessary to get a little vacation from my family, who are pack of venal, heartless grifters who have never done a day's work or spent an honest hour in their lives. Hope that's cool.*

Somehow, she knew exactly how he would react to that. He would tip that hat like they lived in a different century, wish her well, and be on his way. And she didn't think she could bear that.

Kendall corrected herself immediately. What she couldn't bear was the loss of the opportunity this presented, that was all. Her mother and her sister might come looking for her. They usually did, though Kendall had gotten smart since her Rhode Island escape attempt and didn't make such total breaks any longer. Usually she'd call and make it sound like she was doing her own version of the family business on her own. If they got bored they might find her trail, though they were usually too lazy to pay close enough attention to such things. And she always came back in a few days.

It had been longer than a few days now. But one place no member of the Darlington family would think to look for her was in the vicinity of a good, honest man.

Kendall shifted around on the bench seat so she could put her hands on the table. Then she laced her fingers as she held them together, the same way he did.

"I answered your ad because those are the things that I want," she told him, trying to sound as matter of fact as he had. "And I'll be honest, I thought it would be highly unlikely that I'd meet you and think you had them to offer. A lot of people talk, but very few people back up that talking with anything that matters."

He seemed to lean closer, though she didn't feel encroached upon. Quite the opposite. She leaned in too, closing that space between them over that wide wooden table. Like they were both hanging on to each other's every word.

She had to remind herself that she was acting. That this was an *act*.

Though even as she tried to do that, she had to face the fact that it was slightly more complicated than that. Because there was a part of her that wanted to be a woman like the one he was looking for. There was a part of her that wanted nothing else, and so badly that she could still remember exactly where she'd been standing when she'd read his ad. In that rented kitchen in Tacoma. Three or four locations back.

She remembered thinking, *two out of three ain't bad.*

The whole way here, she'd assured herself that she could back out at any point. She'd expected that point would come quickly. She'd almost just stayed in her hotel room, because Marietta seemed like a sweet little spot to escape from life for a while, so why complicate things with some cowboy?

It felt like being on a roller coaster to discover that now, all she wanted to do was convince him that she was the right choice.

"You didn't ask for experience of any kind," she said. She kept her gaze on his, intent and steady. "And that's a good thing, because I don't have any. What I do have is me. I pick up things pretty quickly. I've always been a fast learner. I'm not afraid of hard work, though it would be nice to put that hard work toward building something. I've spent most of my life moving from place to place, wishing I could settle and put down some roots. That's not the kind of thing you can ask a man for on a first date." She thought that sounded a little too serious, so she made herself smile. "Or even the tenth."

Harlan said nothing. He watched her, a fallen angel set into stone, and that roller-coaster ride slipped and dropped, twisted and whirled.

"I'm not opposed to the idea of building up next generations," she continued, keeping her voice as without inflection as she could manage.

She'd laughed about that part, sitting on the bus. A wink and a smile would do the trick there, she'd decided. Men could spend a whole lot of time and energy on a *maybe someday*. Looking at him, however, she had the very distinct impression that this wasn't a man who spent much time flirting. She wasn't sure, in all her life, that she'd ever met a man who made it clear—just by sitting there—that he was about doing the thing or not. No flirting with *maybes*. No *in betweens*.

It was different, that was all. That had to be why her throat was dry.

Kendall hurried on. "In a theoretical sense, I mean. I'm not signing up for a buffet if I haven't even tasted the food." She thought she saw the faintest bit of crinkling in the corners of his eyes, then. And she found she felt emboldened by that. "I think that people have more expectations about marriage than they say they do. What are yours?"

"I'm already married," he told her at once, as if that

didn't require thought. "To the land. To these mountains. Paradise Valley and Montana. I'm a simple man, Kendall. I can't promise you I'll show you far-flung places or buy you pretty things. And not because you don't deserve those pretty things or I can't afford it. But because I come down into town maybe once a week. Usually less, and I'm only here to stock up on supplies. My idea of a good night is getting the paperwork done and going to bed early. If you need tokens to prove affection, I'm going to let you down."

Mayrose would have howled with derisive laughter at that, then left. Breanna would have demanded that he buy her a drink or three for her trouble, then would have tried to see what she could get out of him anyway, because he'd been fool enough to say he could afford it.

Kendall, never one to swim against a rising tide, would have excused herself if they were here and hung back until it was time for damage control.

The thing was, she was a Darlington woman. Darlington women liked their loot. Their little treasures. Trinkets and baubles and any kind of shiny thing. Like magpies on the make.

Until now, Kendall had always assumed that she must too, that it was in her blood. That the only reason she didn't go after her own was that she was too busy managing her mother and sister and their various trails of destruction.

Here in Marietta, Montana, a town she'd never heard of in all her life, she could finally test that theory.

And so she stayed right where she was. Without asking for a drink to ease her troubles.

"What I can promise you is that I will honor you," Harlan continued and it did something to her, to hear him say something like that with that intense gaze of his steady on hers. "I will listen to you. I will do my best to do right by you, to the best of my ability. I might not sing you a sweet song or take you dancing on the weekends, but if you marry me, I will do my best to see to it that we get as close to happy as we can, stay there, and maybe even make some joy out of it while we're at it."

Kendall felt the strangest wash of sensation go through her, then. It was so deep and so wide that for a moment, she thought she might be sick. It took her a long, horrified moment to realize that she wasn't being struck down by a sudden flu. That the burning sensation at the back of her eyes was tears.

She was actually *about to cry*, as if this man had spouted off love poetry.

Something deep inside of her turned inside out, and she was glad she was holding her hands tight together because she could feel a tremor in her fingers. *Darlingtons don't show weakness,* she thought, almost desperately.

But she had the strangest thought that what she really wanted was to reach out to him.

This was all silly, she told herself then, and harshly. Fantasy stuff. She knew better than to believe in fairy tales.

"This isn't how people do things," she said quietly. "Not anymore."

Harlan shrugged. "More folks got together this way than the way they do these days. They knew they didn't have time back then. My great-great-grandfather came out this way, claimed his land, and wrote a letter to his cousin back in Vermont to send him out a wife. He didn't even meet her. She was the youngest girl in a local family and family legend is, she was more adventurous than the rest. She thought it sounded like more fun to go on out into the untamed wilderness and marry a man she'd never met than stay home and wrestle a harsh life out of snowy Vermont with the rest of the family."

"I think I would have liked her." Kendall studied him. "Was she happy?"

"Life isn't supposed to be happy." Harlan said that quietly, but no less intently. "It's life. We have to take into account the good as well as the bad. Understand that things get complicated, plans don't work out, things don't end the way they should. Some winters are so bad they take years to recover from. Sometimes there's heartbreak everywhere you look. That doesn't mean that a life is bad, just that, sometimes, it's hard."

"You're not really selling it," she said, and her voice had gone soft, something she only understood when she heard it.

She had the dizzying thought that this man made her... not recognize herself.

He reached across the table then to place one of his hands over hers, still laced there between them.

And it was like a blinding, white-hot light, but she wasn't blind. All she could see was his hand over hers. More than that, she could *feel* it. His palm was callused and warm and told her more things about this man.

They made him seem *more* honest, more *real*.

Slowly, almost agonizingly, she dragged her gaze up to his.

And the thing about Harlan Carey was, she could feel him everywhere.

It was as if that white-hot lightning bolt blazed out from the point of contact and lit her up, everywhere.

By rights, she should have been ash.

"I'm not a salesman," he told her, like he knew. "What you can depend on is for me to tell it to you straight, like it or not. Whatever it is." The corner of his mouth curled, just slightly. "Some think that's harsh, but I happen to think it's a virtue."

Kendall didn't know what was happening to her then, except that she melted. She simply... pooled into nothing. She felt too hot. She felt flushed and embarrassed, and that was so unlike her that she once again wondered if she was falling ill.

But even if she was, all she could seem to focus on was every beat of her heart that seemed to shudder everywhere inside. That echoing pulse that throbbed in the strangest places from behind her knees to her wrists to an insistent beat between her legs.

She, who had never been rendered wordless in her life, could not think of a single thing to say.

"Are you staying in town tonight?" he asked, in a mild voice at odds with the intent way that dark gaze moved over her.

And his hand was still on hers, telling her how things could be between them. If she agreed. If she really did this. *If,* something in her suggested, *you give up this idea you could ever control a man like him.*

Kendall realized she was just *staring* at him when his mouth crooked. "If you are, I suggest you come on up to the ranch tomorrow and get a feel for the place. Decide one way or the other on this after you've slept on it."

"And then what?" she asked, and it felt like a victory. To get the words out. To say anything at all when there was all of that heat and flush in her throat, the same as everywhere else.

When she still felt half bright light, half ash.

"And then, Kendall Darlington," Harlan drawled in that way she could feel like smoke curling around her bones, his hand still holding hers with just enough pressure to make her shiver all way down her spine, and a gleam in his dark gaze that she could feel like a lick, "assuming we both feel that it's right, we get married."

Chapter Three

KENDALL SLEPT BADLY and woke up groggy and disoriented.

Sunlight poured in through the old windows, illuminating old wood built-ins, bright gilt-edges, and daguerreotypes set on the walls. She bolted upright in the old brass bed with the cloud-soft mattress that had kept her awake because it was *too* lush, *too* nice, *too fancy*—and those things came with a price. Her heart was racing as she looked around, wondering what disaster Mayrose had gotten them into this time.

Because the nicer the hotel room, the more dangerous the game her mother was playing and the more likely it was that Kendall was going to have to find them a way out of it—

She was out of the bed and halfway across the room, all done up in old West splendor, before she remembered.

As far as she knew, Mayrose and Breanna were still back in Idaho.

Or maybe they'd moved on, but they weren't *here*. They didn't do small towns, filled with charm and nosy neighbors who kept track of things that slipped through the cracks in bigger places. There was no way they could be in Marietta unless they'd tracked her here, and she knew that was unlikely.

Not this soon. Not when she hadn't left behind a single clue. She hadn't even asked them what the long-term plan was lately, a question that usually led to extensive theatrics.

Still, it took a long, hot shower to scrub the panic away.

By the time she dressed and made it down to the lobby, however, Kendall was back on form. And that was a good thing, because Harlan Carey was already there, waiting in the lobby.

Though this time, she had the opportunity to observe him before he saw her.

It was immediately clear that she hadn't been imagining the *force* of this man yesterday. He had a kind of commanding presence that was obvious even now, when he was standing over near the doors, engaged in what looked like a pleasant enough conversation with a man much shorter than himself wearing a toothy grin and an officious-looking woman holding a clipboard.

Kendall's initial reaction was to think, *wow, he doesn't like either one of them.*

But the moment she thought that, she made herself stop, then re-examine that conclusion. Why did she think she could read a man she'd only met the day before and knew so little about? That was the kind of thinking that could get a person in trouble.

And Kendall had enough trouble as it was.

As she drew closer, she decided that she didn't really think that it was necessarily because her powers of discernment were so great, though she had certainly had the opportunity to work on them over the years. It was Harlan himself.

He just *looked* as unpretentious and forthright as he'd seemed to her yesterday.

He was dressed the same way as he'd been in Grey's Saloon, in boots and jeans, a nice shirt, and that hat. She realized as she approached that the man he was talking to wasn't necessarily *short*. Not really.

It was just that Harlan himself was so tall.

"Tod," he was saying, sounding like his patience was being tried but was holding steady all the same, "I told you I'd let you know when and if I was ready to sell even one parcel of the land that's been in my family since before yours even knew Montana existed. And I will. But it's not going to be in this lifetime or the next."

It was possible, Kendall thought then, that when he'd told her he was honest to a fault, he'd meant it.

Because he really did seem easy to read, but she didn't think that was because there wasn't a whole lot to read there. He was obviously a man of depths. But he... had nothing to hide.

That was a heady thought.

She almost tripped over her own feet, thinking such a thing. That wasn't the sort of person she usually encountered. Kendall probably would have said, if asked, that such a person didn't exist. *Couldn't* exist.

Harlan shifted his gaze, saw her, and that was headier still.

There was just something about the man. About the way he looked at her. The way he looked at everything with that same intensity.

It made something deep inside of her curl up on itself, as if trying to luxuriate in it. In him.

Kendall wasn't sure this boded well. It was pretty much the opposite of what she'd expected answering that ad would be like, in fact. When she'd imagined it, she'd entertained a whole fantasy that she might be able to do what her family normally did—but more nicely—and spin it out for a while. Give herself a place to lie low and all that.

But she realized, with a start, that it would never have happened that way. If he'd been the kind of man she'd expected, she would have been halfway to Idaho by now. Because she wasn't her family. She never had been and she wasn't now. She cleaned up after them, she didn't play along.

Maybe that was why she'd had so much trouble sleeping.

When he excused himself from his conversation—barely breaking eye contact with her as he stepped around the two people he'd been talking to and made his way directly toward her—she tried desperately to tell herself that since she'd stayed here, she really ought to start thinking strategically.

She had been good at that, at one point. Maybe even yesterday morning, before she'd laid eyes on this man. Though it was hard to remember that—or anything—when Harlan Carey was filling up her entire field of vision.

"Ready?" he asked when he came to a stop before her.

And Kendall felt... flustered. She nodded, because that seemed safer than trying to speak at the moment.

"I realize you don't know me," Harlan continued in that low voice, still with that dark, intense gaze of his trained on her. "Any safeguards you need to put into place so that you feel all right about driving out to the ranch with me are great."

The truly amazing thing, Kendall thought then, was that she hadn't considered safeguards at all. And she should have. If he had been anyone else, she knew she would have.

So now she made a point of typing the address he gave her into her phone, finding it on the map, and then pretending to send it to someone. She tried to imagine what it would be like if there was anyone in her life she could call on in a time of need, or expect to step in and help her in some way...

But there was only Harlan, standing there like he could wait forever if that was what it took her to feel comfortable.

Something inside her shivered. Kendall decided she was done with her little game of pretend. She tucked her phone in her pocket, smiled, and then let him walk her out of the hotel doors toward the street.

Outside, the day was as bright as yesterday had been, but

far warmer. That same vintage truck waited outside the old hotel, gleaming bright red in all the May sunshine.

Kendall couldn't get over the hushed, almost reverent sensation that seemed to hum inside her as he walked her around to the passenger side, opened her door, and made sure she was settled inside before he circled back around to climb behind the wheel.

She didn't want to tell him that no one had ever treated her in a chivalrous manner before. That felt like a deeper conversation, and not one she expected she was going to need to have with this man she might marry, but had no intention of staying with long enough to get *intimate* with.

Something that made her heart seem to hitch in her chest as she thought it, but she refused to pander to it. Because that was the deal, like it or not. That was life.

It was that or let *him* get to know *her*, the oldest Darlington daughter and all that entailed, and that was a hard no.

Harlan started up the truck. He looked over at her with that little crook in the corner of his mouth.

Kendall thought, very distinctly, *this man might be the end of me.*

But whatever that meant, it didn't send her scrambling to let herself out of the truck, so maybe that wasn't the worst thing in the world.

"Did you explore the town?" he asked, very politely. So politely she almost wondered if he could read her—when that should not have been possible. Her own mother and sister claimed she was the most pokerfaced of them all. It was why Kendall always had to run cleanup—she alone could maintain a neutral expression. She alone could keep her thoughts off her face.

"I walked around," she told him, not sure how she managed to sound so calm and very nearly pleasant. "But only a little."

Harlan nodded. Then he took her on the tour of Marietta she'd quickly realized yesterday that she didn't want to give herself.

Because it had been bad enough at a cursory glance when she'd only just arrived. Marietta looked like a postcard, or the sort of storybook she'd found in libraries as a kid and had paged through longingly, wondering if it could be possible some people really got to live like that.

On cheerful streets, bright and happy, while all around spring was beginning to bloom and happy flowers would soon be everywhere.

That was alien enough to a girl used to smokey bars and casinos and the like. But so was the way Harlan talked about this place as he drove her around. The clear and genuine affection she could hear in his tone as he pointed out landmarks and made sure she saw the prettiest views of the town laid out at the foot of Copper Mountain... made her whole body want to shiver, down deep, and keep shivering.

Maybe it did, but she was too busy hanging on Harlan's every word to tell.

He told her about the renovation of the hotel where she was staying. How the Graff had been a wreck until local hero Troy Sheenan decided it was about time a phoenix rose from those ashes. He told her about the Grey family, who'd been running that saloon since they'd erected the first version of it some 125 years ago—the first building that had ever stood in what eventually became Marietta. He drove her down what had to be the prettiest lane Kendall had ever seen, pointing out the Bramble House Inn and the rest of those happy, Victorian homes that it was hard to believe any real people got to live in.

But the more Harlan showed her, the more Kendall began to feel like she was visiting a movie set. She was sure she'd seen at least a few Christmas movies set on what could easily have been Marietta's streets, from the graceful inn to an adorable chocolate shop.

There was a part of her that felt relieved when he headed out of town and into the hills.

As if, were she to stay too long in all that postcard splendor, it would force her to reveal herself. And then he would know who she really was, and she didn't want that.

Not yet, anyway.

Not yet, she thought, more fiercely than she should have.

"My family's ranch has been around almost as long as Marietta has," he told her as he drove into the countryside. Fields behind wooden fences that shouted *the West* to her. Perfect, weathered barns. Horses running in the distance, cows grazing. "I guess because my great-grandfather was a miner, he wasn't worried about the land folks down here in the valley called inhospitable. Because anything is better than a mining shaft."

"I don't have to have spent even one second in a mining shaft to believe that," Kendall agreed.

The old pickup truck ran beautifully as they drove up out of the fields and on to a narrow road that got notably steeper and more treacherous with every mile as it zigged and zagged its way up the side of the mountain that she'd seen from almost every vantage point while down in Marietta proper. It also seemed a lot less springlike, and quickly. There was snow clinging to the mountainside and patches of ice on the road before them whenever they lost the direct sunshine.

But the view as they climbed was spectacular. Mountains sprawled where they liked, and Paradise Valley more than lived up to its name.

And the farther she got from pretty Marietta there at the base of the mountain, the more Kendall could appreciate what a jewel it was—and the better she could breathe. Perfection scared her. She didn't mind admitting it. It was impossible not to wonder what lurked beneath it—or if everyone who belonged in such prettiness could see what lurked in her.

She shoved that off and concentrated on the drive.

"I don't think I'd like to come up this road by foot,"

Kendall said in a particularly slippery stretch. The road ahead looked perilous, particularly as there was only a faint gesture toward a guardrail on the steep side of the road. "Or by horse. Or however people got up mountains back in the day."

"This is Dry Creek Road." Harlan sounded amused. Or maybe it was just that he enjoyed showing his life off. Kendall could imagine that might be fun, if you had one like this. "But no one calls it that. Around here, it's known as Desolation Drive. You don't want to break down here. And you don't want to speed, or hit bad weather, or get disoriented when the snow is coming in sideways. It's not a good place to get stuck."

He looked over at her and she must have had an apprehensive expression on her face—so not her usual neutrality, again, and why was that a thing that was only happening with him?—because he laughed. "Don't worry, Cowboy Point more than makes up for it."

Kendall turned so she could look at him as he drove, looking as relaxed behind the wheel as he had talking to people in the Graff's lobby. Or even sitting across from her yesterday. She had to order herself to force her gaze away from the way he draped one hand over the wheel, because if she thought too much about his hand she would have to think about how it had felt over hers—

That was not the sort of thing she should indulge. Not here in the confines of this vintage truck, making its way up a terrifying road toward a place she had an address to—but no real sense of where it was.

Better not to think about any of that.

"Is your town really called Cowboy Point?" she asked instead, maybe a bit more brightly than called for. "That wasn't on the map you showed me."

"It isn't a town," Harlan replied in that same, steady way, his eyes on the road and the tight turns. "It's more properly an unincorporated community and census designated place." That made his eyes crinkle in the corners. "But it's been called Cowboy Point since the beginning. Out here in the West, we like to name a place so that there's no doubt that— at least once upon a time—it's exactly what it says it is."

She started to respond to him, then paused. "You say that like I'm not from the West myself."

"You have too much of a Southern drawl in your voice to be from the West." Harlan's dark eyes gleamed when she frowned at him. "It's not big and twangy, like Alabama or Texas. Not thick like Mississippi. My money's on Tennessee."

Kendall felt a little bit breathless at that. "As a matter of fact, I spent large parts of my childhood in various suburbs of Nashville." And she didn't like that breathlessness. She didn't like all these odd sensations whirling around inside of her. She cleared her throat. "Tell me more about Cowboy Point."

Because one thing she knew was that people always liked

to tell their stories, if she could get them talking. Always. And the only way she could handle what was happening, what she was doing, was by pretending this was any other normal day. That she was doing the sort of thing she always did. That she was just… gathering the necessary background.

It didn't mean she would stay. It didn't mean she wouldn't.

She was just doing the thing she'd been trained her whole life to do.

"It started off just a few families," he was saying. "Now there's a fair few more. We're considered part of the greater Marietta area, but most of that applies to things like the hospital, the high school. For all intents and purposes, ten miles up a road like this, we're on our own." He lifted a brow her way. "But this is Montana. We like it that way."

Then he returned his attention to the road, and that was a good thing. Because the last bit of the road was even steeper and more winding than before, as they stopped zigzagging up the side of the mountain and actually rounded it.

And once they did, Kendall found herself holding her breath.

Because on the back of Copper Mountain, entirely hidden from the valley down below, was another valley. It was much smaller than Paradise Valley. She could see the whole sweep of it as they drove to the top edge, then began to descend into it through an avenue of Rocky Mountain evergreens that stood like quiet, watchful guardians over a little town that wasn't quite a town.

Either way, there was a collection of buildings clustered in the center of the narrow valley, and houses tucked away along the valley's sides. There was only the one road, no stop signs or stoplights, with dirt roads snaking off here and there. There was an elementary school. A tidy little library. They sat across from each other with a kind of square in the middle, that Kendall imagined must be green in summer. There was a feed store. A general store, according to the sign out front, with what seemed to be a diner attached.

There was a creek running on a diagonal through all this, and despite the name of the road they'd been on, it looked swollen and cold this time of year. There was a bar on the other side.

Across the road, they passed an old, renovated sort of barn that advertised pizza and ice cream. She wondered if they used the big, wide patio in high summer. There were a selection of smaller buildings, old houses dressed up to be businesses and the like, though she couldn't tell what they were.

Kendall had felt as if she was holding her breath the whole time she was in Marietta. It was so perfect that she'd had the bone deep sense that she would break something there, like a bull in a china shop, if she wasn't careful. But Cowboy Point was different.

She felt herself breathe, and deep. And more, she could

almost imagine herself in a place like this, where the air was full of sun and pine and everything looked a little hardier and less manicured than Marietta had. A little tougher, maybe. A little more solitary.

Home, a voice in her pronounced, but she pretended she didn't hear it.

Because that was madness. She'd never had a home. Kendall didn't know what that word meant, not really.

Harlan lifted a few fingers in a lazy wave to the handful of other vehicles they passed, but he kept going until they were climbing up the other side of the small valley, toward the big, old Lodge that sprawled there, facing Copper Mountain.

"This is Cowboy Point Lodge," Harlan told her, slowing to let her marvel at the graceful old building as they passed. "It was called the Jewel of the Rockies, once upon a time, long, long ago. The family that owns it is trying to clean it up again and bring more folks into town, but that, like everything around here, comes with some controversy."

"Doesn't everything," Kendall murmured.

But she was captivated, completely, by the view.

Because right after they passed the Lodge, for a moment, it seemed as if they were perched on the edge of the world.

Behind them, Copper Mountain rose, and the whole of Cowboy Point was tucked up there at the foot of Copper Mountain's snowcapped peak. But laid out before them, she could look out over what seemed like undulating waves toward the horizon, though none of it was water. It was all mountains.

They marched on, one range and then another like some kind of tectonic dance, and she felt sheer exhilaration move through her as if she was dancing too. Because it was one thing to talk about the Rockies. To talk about mountains at all. It was something else again to truly understand how, if you were lucky, looking at them could make your soul feel fresh and new.

Like this was a baptism of sorts, driving into them like this.

She wanted to throw out her arms. She wanted to see if they could *fly*.

Kendall was a little surprised they weren't already, because that was how it felt inside of her. Like they were *soaring* in this little red truck, straight off into the blue.

There was just something about being this far off in a mountain range she knew most people never got to see that made her feel... clean.

A part of her wanted to stay where they were forever, right here where they could see forever on all sides, and just *breathe*.

But Harlan drove deeper into the mountains. Kendall tried to come back into her own skin. He wound his way up the craggy side of a different hill, and as he started down the other side of it, she began to see fences.

"This is the beginning of High Mountain Ranch," he

told her. "We have thousands of acres, stretching almost all the way to Big Sky."

Normally she was more circumspect, but she laughed at that. "And you really had to resort to personal ad?"

Harlan laughed too, and she definitely did not focus too much on how that felt, to laugh *with* him. "It's not that I don't think I could find someone. It's what I told you yesterday. There's a ranch to consider and all things being equal, I'd rather that the business not get tangled up in romantic notions."

"You don't believe in romantic notions?" Kendall did not add that it seemed strange to hear that from him, given that he apparently believed in a kind of chivalry she would have said was dead and buried. Who *opened doors* for a woman these days?

"I believe in them fine," Harlan said, though she thought he sounded different. More measured, maybe. And he kept his gaze on the road. "My parents were high school sweethearts. If my mother hadn't died when I was eight, I reckon they'd be together to this day. Instead, my dad found Belinda, and I got to watch a whole different way to be married and be romantic while you're at it."

"So she's not a wicked stepmother?"

Harlan laughed again. "She's wicked all right. But not to me. Belinda is…" He shook his head. "A whirlwind. It's impossible not to love her."

Kendall couldn't tell what that note was in his voice

then, but it sounded to her like it was possible he might have tried really hard not to love his new stepmother, all the same.

"I don't have anything against romance," Harlan said, as if it was important he make that clear to her. She could feel the touch of that intense stare of his on the side of her face. "But I don't have time for it. I've watched the effort it takes. The care and feeding that it requires, like anything that grows. And the mourning it requires when it dies." She couldn't help but look at him then, at the steady, intent way he was studying her. "When I tell you I'm a practical man, I mean that. In my experience, that's not the kind of attitude that lends itself to any kind of productive dating life."

Kendall ignored the way her pulse beat inside her and tried to imagine that, as he drove her through rolling fields tucked away in these hills, miles upon miles away from anything. She tried to imagine Harlan presenting himself for a regular date. Dinner and a drink, small talk, maybe a little dancing, maybe a walk beneath the stars.

But the images wouldn't come together. Not with a man this direct. This intense.

She felt a kind of shiver move through her again, but it wasn't fear.

It was something else entirely.

Oh no, she thought.

He turned off the road and they were on a dirt lane then, moving slowly up a rolling sort of hillside. She saw outbuildings. Structures she knew had something to do with ranching activities, though she couldn't have said how. And then, in the trees, she began to see the hint of a cabin tucked away here, there. They were spread out quite a ways from each other. One was set up so that it had a view. The next was half-hidden in a grove.

"All of my brothers have cabins on the property," Harlan told her.

"All four of them," she said, remembering.

His mouth crooked. "It seems like more than four, if I'm honest."

The dirt road led them past a proper ranch house within walking distance of more barns, and more outbuildings whose purpose Kendall could only attempt to imagine. "That's the main house. My dad and Belinda live there now."

But he kept on driving, back behind a series of barns and continuing along the lane until they were out of sight of the house. Only then did he pull off, driving up the side of yet another hill before coming to a stop in a clearing.

They both sat there a moment, staring out at the house in front of them.

"I would not call that a cabin," Kendall said. As judiciously as she could.

Harlan leaned forward over the steering wheel, as if looking at the place for the first time. "It *was* a cabin. I just kept adding on to it."

It was an odd little house that should have looked haphazard, but didn't. Like Harlan himself, it had the sense of a ramble—but she suspected that every part of the place served some practical purpose, whether she could tell what it was or not. From the breezeway with a pitched roof that led straight to his own barn to the towering windows everywhere that must let in the mountains and what light there was, it was beautiful.

Like a kind of Rocky Mountain castle, but not flashy. It seemed almost as if it was a part of the trees around it, the mountains on all sides.

"Come on," he said, shooting her a look. "I'll give you a tour."

And now there was no avoiding the reason she was here, looking at his house in the first place. She'd let herself forget it—or she'd kept pushing it away—because the drive had been so pretty. So mesmerizing.

But reality was reality. She knew that better than most. He was giving her a tour because she might actually come and live here.

With him.

In this place that was far, far away from everything she'd ever known, and not just geographically.

It was a little overwhelming, Kendall admitted as she opened her door, then paused as he came around to do it for her. But there was no denying the fact that it was a perfect hiding spot. That there was no possible way her family could find her here. She wasn't sure how they would even begin to look for her here.

That alone would have disposed her to like the place.

But there was also the Harlan of it all.

He showed her around, making a point of indicating that there were separate bedrooms, in case she thought that he was going to insist on husbandly rights immediately. Something she did not find herself as opposed to as perhaps she should have.

But she shoved the notion of *husbandly rights* aside, because a house told a lot of tales about the person who lived in it. And the story of this household was of the same man she'd already met. Measured. Honest.

Everything in the house's structure was masculine, but neat. And not in a way that suggested he'd rushed around last night, cleaning it up. She got the sense that Harlan was not a man who liked clutter. The things he had looked cared for. Comfortable.

Useful, not fanciful.

Like him.

Like me, she thought.

They stopped in the main room that had a big fireplace tucked into a stone chimney that divided the living room and the kitchen. Kendall tried to think of the last time she'd spent any real amount of time in a house. It was usually hotels. Apartments. Rented places that were easily left behind.

This was a house with a deep foundation. With roots.

She could feel it.

And then there was that gleaming thing in his dark gaze. Kendall could feel the echo of it deep inside of her.

This could be home, a voice inside her whispered, the way it had in Cowboy Point proper. *At last.*

And that was dangerous. So dangerous. She knew it. She could *feel* it, crackling along her skin and under it, like electricity.

"I'm surprised you have time to take me on a tour like this," she said, holding his gaze, because she could be steady too. "I thought the whole point of this was that you don't have that kind of time."

"I'm not an animal, Kendall," he said, and she was beginning to understand that tone of his. That it was him being funny. Or something like sardonic, but without any dark edge.

She was beginning to understand, further, that she liked it.

Given precious little encouragement, she might like him, too.

"Good to know," she replied.

He didn't smile with his mouth but she saw it all over him, just the same. "I might want a wife in an unconventional way. But I don't want that wife to be uncomfortable. I don't want it to seem like I don't care about how we'll get on. Because I do." She saw something on his face then. Some kind of resolve. "From my perspective, I think that this could work. So it's really down to you."

Kendall thought about what that might mean. All the things that it might mean. Because there was the house. And what she imagined the work would be like. There was also that bit about the next generation, about *husbandly duties*, that she'd assumed she'd try to avoid.

Before she'd met him, that was.

Though she stopped herself. Because she wasn't going to be here that long, surely.

And for the first time since she'd gotten rid of her panic attack this morning, she felt a kind of desolation move through her and settle in, hard. She couldn't let herself think about her inevitable departure. Or ask herself why, exactly, it should hit her that way.

Instead, she looked at Harlan Carey, who made her feel things when she had long since come to believe that she was incapable of feeling anything.

That seemed like enough.

And in this beautiful house, hidden so far away from the world, who knew? Maybe she would have time for all kinds of things before her past caught up with her.

But she didn't tell him all that. What she did instead was smile at him.

Because this wasn't meant to be a measured decision. It was meant to be impulsive. It was meant to be based on practicality alone.

And practically speaking, she could live here quite happily. He seemed decent enough. And Lord knew, she'd seen enough of the opposite kind to last a lifetime.

There wasn't going to be time to get to know him. That was the point.

This was the way people had been doing things like this since the dawn of time, she knew.

Maybe it was better. Safer, really. If all you had practical considerations, anything else could be gravy if it came along.

And if it didn't work out that way, she could leave.

She told herself that was why it was so easy to smile at him the way she did, and let it widen when he smiled back.

"Well?" she asked. "Are you going to propose or am I?"

Chapter Four

H ARLAN DID THE proposing.
Obviously.

"Will you marry me, Kendall?" he asked, quietly, of the woman who stood there in the house he'd built with his own hands, sweat, and muscle.

And maybe it was a trick of the spring light, but it almost felt like she'd always been meant to be here. With him. It was almost like he'd built all of this for her.

It almost feels like fate, he thought, but he brushed that off.

He'd never spent too much time worrying about things like proposals. Or fate, for that matter. There had never been a reason to concern himself with such things, but now there was Kendall.

And while she stood there and gazed back at him and he truly didn't know how she was going to answer, he understood that he was far more invested in marrying *her*—not just in marrying, but in marrying her *specifically*—than he'd realized.

He wasn't sure how that had happened. He only knew it had.

Kendall cleared her throat. Her gaze was locked to his.

Harlan had the strangest notion that this was something sacred, this stolen moment here in his house. This moment that hadn't come around the way such moments were meant to, maybe, but here they both were all the same.

"Yes," she said, right when he was about to wonder if she was going to answer at all. And about to have to face how he was likely to feel about it if she didn't. Or if she said no. "I'd like that."

And then they were both grinning at each other like they'd won something.

They celebrated their arrangement by getting back in his truck, driving off the mountain, then heading into Bozeman to get themselves a marriage license. While they were at it, they set a wedding date with the judge for two days later.

Harlan bought her a ring on the way out of town, a pretty sapphire that she said made her think of the big, blue Montana sky over all the mountains, and he caught her looking at it as they drove back down the highway toward Marietta again. Twisting it this way and that like she was trying to see how it caught the light.

It was funny how this thing they were really, truly doing was settling in him like an inevitability.

Like he'd wanted Kendall for a long time when he'd only met her yesterday.

Wisely, he kept that to himself.

It didn't seem to make any sense for her to keep staying

at the Graff when they'd decided to go ahead and do this thing. They both agreed. So they checked her out when they got to Marietta, packed her two small bags into his truck, and installed her in the spare bedroom of her choice in his house on the ranch.

"Why did you build so many bedrooms when you live alone?" she asked after he'd set her suitcases neatly beside the bed she'd chosen and they'd both stared at the bed, then at each other, and had retreated back out into the living room without looking at each other like that again.

Not until they were sitting there across the coffee table from each other like company.

She'd looked at all of the rooms he had and had chosen the one on the far side of the house from his—though he didn't think the distance from him was why she'd picked it. Watching her make her choice, he was pretty sure that her choice revolved around the view. And that back bedroom had a good one of nothing but mountain ranges marching off into the wild blue yonder.

He'd watched her curl her fingers on her left hand, as if connecting that view to her ring.

And had been surprised at the tugging sensation he'd felt then, deep inside, like he was connecting to those things, and her, just the same.

"I've always intended to have a family," he told her now, more formally. Because it was strange how it felt to say that out loud when the woman he was going to marry, and presumably make that family with, was sitting there in front of him. Right here in this house where he expected that family would live. After they got to know each other a whole lot better than they did today. Imagining all of that, thinking about what was to come, made that tugging thing inside seem to go deeper still. "I guess I like to prepare."

Kendall gazed back at him, and he thought he saw warmth there. Or he wanted to see it. "There's nothing wrong with that."

And it had been a long day of neglecting the ranch—he'd told his family he had a doctor's appointment so they wouldn't come looking for him or question why he wasn't doing the things he normally did—so he took her with him when he went back out to see to his usual chores. She watched everything he did intently as he went about the typical evening routine. She asked good questions about the stock and the land, and when they got back to his house, she told him that if he was okay with letting her find her way around his kitchen, she would be happy to cook.

"For the record, I know how to cook," Harlan told her as they walked from his truck to the house. *Their* house now, he corrected himself, and wasn't that an odd little switch. It set off that tugging thing inside again. "I don't expect you to move in here and become a maid." He considered that. "Or a housekeeper of any kind. I just want to clarify that."

"That's good." Kendall regarded him solemnly once they were inside, toeing off their shoes in the foyer that functioned as a mud room and kept the ranch out of the house. She nodded through to the living room and the kitchen beyond. "It looks like you keep this place cleaner than I ever would. Though I'll try to keep up." She stuck her hands in the pockets of her jeans, adjusting her left hand when her ring caught. "I'm used to moving around a lot. It sounds like fun to settle into a kitchen and see what I can do with it, that's all. Besides, I'm hungry. Aren't you?"

"Famished," he agreed.

Harlan washed up, then went to get the fire going before the dark settled in and the temperature dropped as low as it usually did, and no matter that it was supposedly springtime. At this elevation warmer weather was always a gift, never a given. While he worked on getting the blaze going, he was acutely aware of Kendall moving around in the kitchen on the other side of the chimney, opening cabinets and the fridge, then banging the pots around.

He'd already showed her the freezer in the garage that was really more of a workshop for the various projects that always cropped up around here. But it was also where he stored enough meat to feed an army or two, because the Careys were cattle people. There was always beef on hand.

Kendall had laughed when he'd told her that, far out in one of the more remote pastures where his father had once kept alpacas. *Sweet talker,* she'd teased him.

He moved to the kitchen doorway and had a sudden, old memory that bled into two memories that overlapped each other. The first when he was just a little boy, lying on the floor in front of the big fire over in the main house while his mother made the same sort of happy, meal-making noises in the kitchen there. He couldn't have been more than six, and that meant it would be a good year yet before they knew she was sick.

His father had preferred to put his feet up after a long day on the ranch, or maybe Alice had wanted a few moments to herself. But Zeke would watch the news, muttering back at the newscasters, while Harlan flipped importantly through his picture books and the twins knocked down each other's Lego castles and usually, also, each other.

Fast-forward about ten years to the second memory and Harlan was at the kitchen table of that same kitchen, focused on his schoolwork on those late evenings after the bus dropped him and the rest of the kids from Cowboy Point off at the General Store. By the time he made it home, Belinda was always in the finishing stages of making dinner. And his father didn't sit and watch television. He was always handling Boone and Knox—who were technically Harlan's half brothers, though no one had ever used the word *half* to describe anything in their family—or barking at the twins to stop their MMA matches all over the house.

Two sides of a coin, he thought now, remembering both of those typical family evenings. Or the memories were more like a choice laid out before him. He had the distinct impression that what he did tonight could set a precedent for all the nights to come.

That all these moments mattered, because they didn't know each other. Because they didn't have a history to refer back to. Because this was, technically, a second date—and here she was moved in and making dinner.

He didn't mind the pace. But he knew he was auditioning for a third date that could go bad—that being their marriage—if he wasn't careful.

Luckily, Harlan had always been careful. So careful and deliberate that Wilder and Ryder spent every moment they weren't battling each other throughout their childhood making fun of him for it.

The more you mock me, he'd told them when he was all of sixteen, *the more I know that everything I'm doing is right.*

Not that such statements had deterred them.

Harlan didn't go and sit in the living room to watch the news the way his dad had when he was little, and not because he was putting on a show for his brand-new fiancée. But because he never did that. He didn't like to watch the news—any news—because he preferred to form his own opinions from facts. Not from other people's spin on those facts.

He felt the same way about the gossip machine that fueled their little valley, and would no doubt already be churning, because he was certain at least one of his neighbors had seen him driving by with *a woman* in his truck.

But that was an issue for the future.

Tonight he settled in at the table he'd fashioned from reclaimed wood he'd found around the property and could remember how gangly he'd felt as a teenager. How uncomfortable in his own skin. Funny how having a pretty woman in the house made him feel that way all over again.

"How do you form an opinion?" he asked Kendall as she assembled ingredients on the counter, looking through his cabinets with the air of a person on a journey of discovery. As if she was building her own map of his spice rack in her head, and was fascinated by what she came across along the way.

"I've always found that it was best to keep my opinions to myself." She glanced back over her shoulder at him, her eyebrows rising in a way that reminded him of that moment he'd first seen her. The way she'd tipped up her chin in defiance as she'd walked across the saloon toward him. "Or are you anticipating the kind of marriage where you tell me what my opinions ought to be?"

Harlan laughed at that. "Sounds pretty boring. I like a steady kind of life, because nothing that happens on the ranch is ever *steady* so it makes a nice change when my homelife is, but I can't say I'm partial to *boring*."

And he thought he saw her smile before she looked down and set about slicing up vegetables, then throwing them into the same big saucepan she'd set on one of the burners.

"A lot of men prefer that a woman mirror back their thoughts and opinions, and keep her own to herself,"

Kendall said mildly.

Harlan watched her as she moved around the warm kitchen that looked brighter than it ought to, with her in the middle of it. She took out flour and a few other ingredients and he watched as she made a quick sort of dough, then put it in the oven.

And only when she'd cleaned that up did she go and take a package of thawed beef out of his fridge that he'd figured he'd make into a few burgers, then start browning it in the spices she'd assembled.

"Is that what you're running from?" he asked her. "A life like that?"

She shot him a look, but then returned her attention to putting all the pieces of the meal she had thrown together into the big saucepan once the meat was drained and ready. "What I'm looking for," she said—very carefully, to his ear, "is the kind of partnership you mentioned before. Where my opinions and contributions are valued. I think everyone's going for that, don't you?"

Harlan thought about his brothers, who worked the land because they felt like they were a part of it. Because while Harlan, as the oldest, had been put "in charge" of their generation from a young age, they all knew that none of this belonged to him. It was *theirs*.

When Zeke passed on—and he winced, not wanting to think about that too closely, or the fact that far-off day was closer than it should have been—it would belong to all of them equally.

It mattered. Belonging mattered. He tried to think what it would be like not to feel so rooted to this place. To this particular stretch of land. To his brothers and the mountains, as if they were all part and parcel of the same thing.

Because, he supposed, they were. Careys had been here so long they might as well be geological.

He didn't have it in him to be quite so imaginative, he found, no matter how hard he tried. He was rooted too deep, right here where he'd always been, and he liked it that way.

"Why did you move around so much?" he asked her instead.

Kendall pulled the bread she'd made out of the oven and cut it up, then brought it over to the table on a plate. She put out the crock of fresh butter from his brother Boone's dairy cows beside it.

Then she went over and ladled out huge helpings of the meal she made and brought that over too, pulling up her own chair at his table.

Harlan was used to living alone. He enjoyed his own company. His brothers liked to poke at him about it, but he always pointed out that having all of them in his face all the time was *why* he liked being on his own.

But this was better, despite that *tugging*, deep within. Or maybe because of it.

"Call it a chili soup," she said, wrinkling up her nose as she looked down at her bowl. "It would have to sit longer, and thicken, to be chili. But it works well as a soup, too."

"I don't care what you call it. It smells fantastic."

It tasted better still.

And it didn't occur to him until the next morning when he was out in the cold, doing his usual chores before dawn, that she had never answered that question about why she'd moved around so much.

Deliberately, he was inclined to think.

They drove back up to Bozeman on the appointed day and got married in as economical a fashion as possible. Kendall wore a dress. It was light green and made her legs the focal point, which he couldn't complain about. Harlan wore his best jeans, his fanciest boots, and the cowboy hat he kept for special occasions.

There was a quick little ceremony before the judge. And all he could remember of it, afterward, was that kiss.

That brief little kiss.

The way her eyes had met his, somehow hot and solemn at once. How she'd moved close and he'd let her set the pace of it, waiting as she lifted up on her tiptoes to brush her lips across his.

Damned if he didn't feel it all the way down to his toes, a kind of humming that set up shop there, like it was never going away.

And the funniest part was that he didn't mind.

He tried to shake it off. Or stop focusing on it, anyway. On the way home, he asked if she wanted to stop in Livingston to have a celebratory kind of meal, but Kendall looked at him from the passenger side of his truck, busy putting her hair up on the top of her head.

"Surely there's work that needs doing back at the ranch," she said.

"You are a girl after my own heart, Kendall Darlington," he told her as she finished tying her hair into a knot and settled back against the seat.

"Kendall Carey," she corrected him, and then laughed. "I think it's almost completely official. I have to send in a few forms, that's all."

Then they sat there as they drove down into the splendor of Paradise Valley in what felt like a companionable enough quiet. Harlan, for his part, found himself thinking about the fact she'd changed her name. Or was planning to change it.

They hadn't discussed it. And he hadn't known, until that very moment, how much he was going to like the fact that she'd gone ahead and done it anyway.

He would have said that a name wasn't particularly important.

But he liked his on her all the same.

They spent the next couple of days getting used to each other, inside the house and out. The simple fact of another person in the same space took some adjustment, though Harlan found he liked it. What he couldn't tell was where the line was for her—was she being careful because this was new? Or was she… jumpy?

On Sunday, Harlan figured it was high time he introduced his family to his wife.

"You didn't tell them you were getting married?" Kendall asked in astonishment on the drive down to the main house that Sunday afternoon. "I... don't know how to respond to that."

"I told you that my father made his announcement." Harlan felt almost defensive, and that was unusual for him. He typically stood behind his own decisions one hundred percent, no matter what anyone else thought. "They've all met me. They should have expected I would get moving on it as soon as possible."

"Exactly how competitive are you with your brothers?" she asked after a moment, frowning at him, but more like she was trying to figure him out than anything else.

"I'm not competitive with them at all," Harlan said. But then he grinned. "Because I always win."

Kendall laughed, and he realized once she did that he'd wanted that. That it mattered to him that she was happy. That this was working for her, this marriage thing.

Maybe what mattered was her, plain and simple.

And part of this was that he had to consider the choices he made, the hows and the whys of it all, in the new light, didn't he? Because he had to explain what he did to the woman beside him and he wasn't sure how to do that. He didn't know how to tell her that he hadn't told anyone she was coming. That he hadn't considered it and more, he hadn't told anyone about her at all.

He *wanted* to drop a bomb.

And he wasn't sure he could articulate why.

"I need to make a confession," he told her as he parked outside the main house in his usual spot.

"Already?" Kendall shook her head, but she didn't sound concerned. "We haven't been married a whole weekend yet."

"They not only don't know we're married, they don't know you're coming at all," Harlan told her. "I didn't tell them I was out looking for a wife. Or how I went about it. Or that I met you."

He didn't know what he expected by way of a reaction. He figured most women would get a little upset. And rightly.

But Kendall eyed him in that way of hers, as if he was a set of mathematical equations that never added up to the same thing. "Maybe you should tell me what you're hoping to get out of Sunday dinner today. That way I can try to help you get it."

"You don't have to do anything but be married to me."

Funny how that sat there between them like some kind of vow. And echoed inside his body like that kiss again, a deep, reverent hum that made his bones ache.

"I don't have a big family," she told him, after letting his words sit there a moment. "I don't have any brothers. Just one sister and a pack of girl cousins we avoid. But somehow, I think it's going to be a little more complicated than that."

"Maybe so," Harlan conceded. "But that's on me."

"That's on us," she countered. "We're either a team or we're not, Harlan."

"I guess it's time to find out." And he watched, bemused and touched in a way he couldn't explain, as she reached out and very gently touched her fist to his. "Is that... a secret handshake?"

"It doesn't have to be a secret." Kendall smiled at him and that humming in him shifted into a full song. "I just think that some things require a little more punctuation."

Harlan could see from the collection of trucks that they were the last ones here. That alone would have been worthy of comment from the rest of his family. He was always the one who said that being on time was ten minutes late.

He couldn't have been more of the eldest son if he tried.

As they walked across the yard for the door, he took Kendall's hand in his. And he flashed back, instantly, to that moment down in Grey's Saloon when he'd covered her hand with his and felt it like an electric charge.

It was the same now.

It was the same, but brighter. Hotter.

And it was its own melody, weaving into that song in him and making him wonder how a man could possibly be expected to keep all of that inside.

He caught her looking at the place where their hands were joined, then up at him, and that electric charge almost seemed to shimmer in the air between them, out in the yard beside his childhood home.

Harlan found himself wondering about things he'd tried to keep firmly on the back burner, because they weren't supposed to be the point. Or not so soon, anyway.

How she would taste, for example.

Not just that mouth of hers that he was pretty sure he'd dreamed about, but all the rest of her, too. When he thought about Kendall, when he watched her move, he found that the way he wanted her was… comprehensive.

He was a methodical man.

And Harlan couldn't think of anything he wanted more than to practice his form of methodology on her.

Inch by inch, until they were both shaking.

But he was prepared to wait for that. As long as it took.

Here, now, there was an entirely different gauntlet to run.

He led her inside, into this house that never changed. Oh, maybe there were different pictures on the walls than the ones he remembered from when he was a kid. But still smelled like the same house, like sunlight and butter, wood and earth. The light and shadow still chased each other through the airy rooms the way they always had.

And he could hear his brothers' voices from the kitchen in back, tangling together in the usual mixture of laughter and good-natured complaint.

Harlan held on to her hand as he took her with him through the house, not letting her stop to look closely at the pictures showing him in various states of youth. There would be time for that. Or, maybe there would never be time, because he wasn't sure he needed her looking at him, toothless and proud as a little kid in his daddy's cowboy hat and nothing else.

It hadn't occurred to him to get out ahead of those sorts of embarrassments. He'd never brought a woman here before.

But it was too late now. Everyone was in the kitchen. This was happening.

And he really was going to have to ask himself why, exactly, he'd decided to do this in the most dramatic way possible.

Not now, he told himself.

He took Kendall to the arched entrance into the rambling kitchen that opened up to fields and mountains and, closer in, the vegetable garden, and waited there.

For a moment, no one looked up.

Belinda was at the stove, and whacked Zeke's hand with a wooden spoon when he tried to grab a tidbit from the roast. His brothers, the three of them that lived here and were in town this weekend, were sprawled around the kitchen table looking like various versions of the same general theme. All tall. All rangy. All dark blond, though Harlan and the twins had dark eyes like their mother, while Boone and Knox had a darker version of Belinda's hazel eyes that tended toward gold when she was happy and copper when she was mad.

He knew the exact moment everything went still.

The quiet rolled out while, one by one, everyone turned to look.

To stare.

And Harlan had always prided himself on being the very opposite of theatrical, an accomplishment in a family like his.

But he sure had set this up for maximum drama, hadn't he?

And there was still no time to question it. It was done.

"Hope we can set another place at the table," he drawled, and enjoyed the way everyone stared at Kendall, then back again at him. "I'd like to introduce you all to Kendall. My wife."

And then, bomb dropped, Harlan settled back to enjoy the first mess he'd made in his long career of otherwise entirely blameless behavior.

Because it turned out, it felt real good.

Chapter Five

A T SOME POINT Kendall was going to have to really think about why it was that Harlan had decided *this* was the way to make an introduction. Why he'd thought it would be a good idea to surprise his entire family with a whole *wife*.

She told herself it wasn't about her, because it couldn't be. She hadn't known the man a week. They'd been in touch only a little longer than that.

Nonetheless, no matter who it was about, she had to jump in.

Because it was that or… sink into the floor.

For a moment, his entire family seemed to be frozen in shock, staring back at the two of them as if they didn't entirely comprehend what Harlan had said. She took in the crowd of people, mostly men, in the room—and she told herself it was the growing hysteria inside her that made her imagine the number of them was expanding by the second—and the way they looked from Harlan to her. Then down to their clasped hands, which she hadn't exactly had time to adjust to either.

This went on for what seemed to her to be an eternity or two, and she couldn't take it.

"It's so nice to meet you all," Kendall said merrily, before she combusted. "But I'm guessing that this is something of a surprise."

The woman at the stove broke first. She threw up her hands, cried out something in what sounded like Spanish, and then came barreling over. She wiped her hands on her apron as she came. A tiny sort of woman, all curves and flashing gold eyes, she grabbed Kendall to her heart as if she'd been waiting her whole life for this moment.

And in doing it, somehow gave the impression that she would have chosen Kendall for Harlan if she'd been consulted.

"I'm sorry that no one in this house has a single manner between them," she said when she released Kendall from that first, surprisingly welcoming hug. And Kendall, who was not used to hugs at all and certainly not *pleasant* or *welcoming* ones, could only stand there dumbly. Luckily, this did not seem to matter. "I'm Belinda. I'm Harlan's stepmother and clearly he has secretly hated me all this time, because why else would he want to give me this heart attack?" She stepped back, squeezing Kendall as she went, and then turned on Harlan. "Married? You got *married*? How is this possible when not one of us was invited to the wedding?"

Though she glared around the room as if she wasn't sure about that, and was checking to see if more betrayals had occurred.

"It wasn't the kind of thing that needed a crowd," Har-

Ian said, and he looked calmer than ever in the midst of what was clearly a whole lot of family emotion and reaction. Kendall filed that away, too, because it was more interesting information about this man she'd married so quickly.

It turned out that she was... thirsty for as much information about Harlan as she could get.

Kendall told herself that was just smart on her part. Didn't they say information was power? She'd never had much of that, but she knew it couldn't hurt.

Harlan tugged her close to him, so that the rest of the tall, brawny men in the room could stop looking like a huge crowd and simply be his brothers—because they couldn't be anyone else.

"I'm Wilder," said the tallest of them with an easy sort of grin that indicated he, too, recognized an awkward moment and was enjoying it, the same as Harlan. Wilder looked as if someone had taken Harlan and figured out how to make all that ruggedness a little bit prettier, a whole lot wickeder, and the kind of dangerous that made a woman look twice despite herself. *Wow*, Kendall thought, and inched even closer to Harlan. "If you ever happen to see someone wandering around who looks like me, but much uglier and notably less charming, that would be my twin, Ryder. Though currently he's off at the rodeo."

"I'll keep that in mind. Ryder, the ugly twin."

"Exactly." Wilder grinned. "Feel free to use that as a nickname when you meet him."

"I'm Boone," said the next brother. He was about Harlan's height, but he was built like a brick house. Like he could knock structures down with a single glance, and maybe a mountain or two if he got his shoulder into it. "And I can see why Harlan wanted to keep you a secret. He never did like competition."

"In order to compete," drawled the brother beside him, "you'd have to stop mooning around over your best friend, wouldn't you, Boone?" He laughed when Boone scowled at him and reached over the table to shake Kendall's free hand. "I'm Knox. I'm the baby of the family. They'll tell you I'm spoiled but they're ornery and jealous because they had to earn their love. I just get it, free of charge."

"More like free of consequences," Harlan growled. "Kendall, they're all liars. You should know that before you listen to anything they might tell you about me."

"We're not going to scare her away," Wilder said with a roll of his eyes. "We've been trying to convince someone to put up with you for years."

Boone nodded. "Never thought we'd see the day."

"We tried a reward, but no one took us up on it," Knox said sadly. "They've all met him."

Harlan looked down at Kendall. "What did I tell you?"

Kendall laughed, then again as he guided her away from the little scrum of his brothers and toward the older man who stood by the stove. She knew who he was immediately. He looked the way she imagined Harlan would, sometime in the future. His hair was gray but his eyes were bright, and he stood tall and strong.

Kendall thought that he didn't look the slightest bit sick, but she knew better than to say something like that.

"This is my father," Harlan told her. "Dad, this is my wife, Kendall. Behave."

"My son thinks his brothers' wild behavior comes from me," the old man rasped, also reaching over to shake hands. His grip was firm and friendly. "I don't know how to tell him it's in reaction to how uptight he is."

"Don't worry," Kendall said with a wink. "I'll be sure to make that clear."

"Harlan could use a little positive reinforcement from time to time," Zeke said, with a bland look toward his eldest son. "Otherwise he gets a little testy."

"More than a little," came Boone's voice.

"Are we calling it *testy?*" queried Knox. "I thought *anal retentive* was more on point."

"Don't scare off the only woman who's ever given the bastard a chance," Wilder chided them. "Who knows when he can trick another one into giving him the time of day?"

Harlan rolled his eyes at all of them, and helped himself to a stolen bite of the roast that his father had gotten swatted at for attempting. "Idiots."

And it was fascinating, Kendall thought as the conversation swelled once again, to have spent a little time getting to know someone only to see, here in this kitchen and around the huge table that dominated it, an entirely different way that he was known.

It was more fascinating that he had expected this reception, seemed unbothered by it, and seemed perfectly happy to let her see him here. Surrounded by a family that did not treat him with any kind of reverence whatsoever.

She found it refreshing, coming as she was from a life filled with so many theatrical productions in place of actual relationships.

More than that, it was a particular sort of treat to sit in the middle of a family that seemed to *enjoy* each other so much. Oh, sure, there was grumbling. There were complaints. They clearly all took tremendous joy in giving each other a hard time, and whatever one of them gave out, they got it back even harder.

Belinda included.

Yet what struck her the most was that all of it was done with laughter.

They poked at each other. They sat around the table with huge platters of food and settled in like they had nowhere else to be and nothing else to do. As if it was the highlight of their week to gather together like this.

And Kendall knew perfectly well how to talk to people. It was a skill like any other and she'd always been good at it. So she wasn't sure when it occurred to her that she wasn't playing a role here.

All the brothers were going back for seconds and thirds,

and she was asking them questions about their lives, and not only because that was the easiest way to get people talking. Strangely enough, she found that she really wanted to know the answers.

She learned that Belinda had grown up in California, though everyone at the table muttered about as if she'd said she grew up with a plague. She discovered that Zeke had been an only child, which was why he'd made sure to have a big family himself.

"You need to make sure you have that free labor," he drawled.

She found out that Wilder missed his twin, though he was proud of him, and would obviously deny he'd ever said that out loud. That Boone had branched off from the family's main ranching concern and had started his own dairy, with a little farming thrown in. Just to see what he could do. That Knox was the only member of the family with an agriculture degree, though of all of them, he was the one who deflected her questions and acted like the only thing he'd done at the University of Montana over in Missoula was play a little football and drink.

And despite all the brothers giving him a hard time, they all clearly adored Harlan.

It made her feel warm all over, as if that was somehow a reflection on her, too.

They were all so alike, these brothers and their father. All these different versions of the stranger she'd married, and seeing them together like this allowed her to see the different facets in him.

She wasn't playing a role when she rose to clear the plates when everyone had finished eating. Kendall wasn't trying to ingratiate herself, she just wanted to help.

Or maybe be a part of this family too, in the only way she could.

Though she didn't really think anything of it until she was standing by the sink, getting a start on the washing up.

"Guests don't do dishes," Zeke told her in that raspy voice of his. "That's a house rule, I'm afraid."

Kendall shot the old man a look. "I married your son. I think that makes me not a guest, by definition."

Zeke grinned, then settled in to help dry. And by the time they finished, Belinda had taken three pies out of the oven and laid them out down the center of the table.

Knox followed after her, plunking down cartons of vanilla ice cream at intervals.

And then Kendall watched as these grown men threw themselves into their dessert as if they hadn't eaten all day, when she just seen them all polish away a giant roast, trays of potatoes, and thick pieces of freshly baked bread.

"Believe it or not," Belinda said dryly, watching Kendall's reaction, "they ate a lot more when they were teenagers. This is the pack of them slowing down with age."

That set off a debate all its own. About what skills they'd already lost because they weren't teenagers any longer. And how it was that Harlan could not only be the oldest of them all, but already have taken on the characteristics of a geriatric old man. At least according to the rest of them.

"A geriatric old man who can kick your ass," her husband replied, almost lazily. "All your asses, in a row."

After dessert, Kendall helped clean up the kitchen, but all the brothers trooped out to one of the barns to consult about something having to do with hay. Or maybe it was horses. Or maybe it was time for bodies to cash checks made by smart mouths.

Because when they came back a while later, it was clear that there had been a few wrestling ass-kickings, if the hay on the back of shirts and the smirks on faces were anything to go by.

"Did you actually wrestle?" she asked Harlan when they climbed back in his truck.

"They wish," he said with a laugh. "They've been trying to take me down their whole lives. They're still trying."

But he looked smug when he said it.

She had a million questions to ask him, because she wanted to know... everything. She had never had such an up, close, and personal connection with a family that wasn't already rotten, hemorrhaging, and in its death throes.

Thinking back, she'd never really been around people like the Careys before. People whose care for each other beamed out bright in everything they did and said. Who would, she had absolutely no doubt, squabble with each other until the end of time but be the first to defend each other against any comers.

It made a funny sort of feeling settle deep in her gut, as if her own nervous system didn't know how to handle what that meant. Or that kind of love that, until today, she'd always believed was a myth.

Something for TV shows and movies, where problems could be solved in an hour or two, and no matter what happened, people loved each other the whole way through.

Fairy tales, she'd always thought.

But before Kendall could really commit to that spiral, she noticed that Harlan was headed the opposite way from his house. He took the dirt road that wound back down through the ranch and all around, as if they were on their way back to Marietta.

"I thought I'd take you on a little tour of Cowboy Point," Harlan said, reading the questions she didn't ask him in the way she looked over at him. "Give you a lay of the land."

"Do I need a lay of the land?"

"You do." He looked at her as the truck bumped over a rough patch in the road. "Because you can't be comfortable in a place you don't know, can you?"

Kendall had a lump in her throat, suddenly, and she didn't know why. She nodded, then looked out the window, hoping that whatever emotion was gripping her would fade.

And the same way as always, she was struck by the beauty

of the landscape immediately, like a different sort of emotion altogether. By the mountains rolling out all around them and the fact that for miles and miles and miles, there was no one else around.

Just the two of them in Harlan's old red truck, with a bright sky above them and mountains that were still clinging on to the remnants of winter.

Slowly, she found that the lump in her throat dissolved. And she could breathe normally without worrying that any moment, a rogue sob might break free.

He slowed as he crested the hill where the old Lodge he'd shown her sat and nodded up at it again. "To catch you up on the history around here, the Lodge is owned by the Stark family. The Stark brothers, whose names you might see on all kinds of things around here, are getting on now. They're the reason the Lodge got into such bad shape. The three of them couldn't agree on a thing and it fell to pieces while they argued. Now it's up to the cousins, their kids, to see if they can put it all back together again."

Kendall gazed up at the old building. She didn't have to know any history to see the possibilities in the graceful lines of the place. In the windows and the grand porches that needed no adornment with such a stunning view in all directions. "You think they'll do it?"

Harlan made a low sound that wasn't quite a laugh, more a sound of acknowledgment. "Jack Stark is the oldest cousin. I've never known him to fail at anything." His dark eyes gleamed when he caught her gaze. "We played football together in high school. I wouldn't bet against him."

He drove her down into the little valley that was Cowboy Point, and Kendall was sure that in the few days she'd been here it was already changing into the new season. There were buds on the trees, new flowers opening in tidy yards, and green coming in everywhere. The graceful avenue of all those tall pines stretched toward the sky and the sun danced down between their branches, making Kendall feel something like *dazzled*.

As if this place was enchanted.

Maybe it was, because there were people strolling down the road as if... that was a thing people did. Eat a Sunday dinner, have a Sunday drive, top it off with a Sunday stroll. That was astonishing enough.

But Kendall saw that everybody waved at Harlan as he drove by. That hadn't been an aberration that first day, or just his friends. Everybody here knew him, or his truck. Everybody here waved, at everybody else. And he lifted his hand in reply as he drove her down the main strip again, pointing out the same few places she'd seen before. But always in terms of the families involved and the members of those families he knew.

As if he was engaged in an ongoing conversation with all these people. All these neighbors and friends.

This place, Kendall thought, was its own fairy tale.

He took one of the side roads that wound out toward the

creek, where she could see the bar in the distance, but also the small church tucked away closer to the woods.

"I don't know your take on the hereafter," Harlan said when she looked at him, not sure what his aim was. "I thought you should know where the church was, anyway. Not too far from the bar, of course." Again, the gleam of dark eyes and amusement from beneath his cowboy hat. "Montanans are practical like that."

Kendall didn't know how to tell him the Darlingtons avoided sacred spaces, lest they be struck down from on high upon entry. She only nodded, not sure why her throat was tight again. Maybe she liked the idea that this man wasn't only concerned with the roof over her head and the food she might eat, but her immortal soul as well.

When the people who should have loved her best were only concerned with what she could do for them.

That was such an oddly heady—and heavy—thought that it took her a while to recognize that he was driving them back through town so slowly that it had to be deliberate. A wave here, a wave there, and a whole lot of curious looks aimed at Kendall in the passenger seat.

"Are you giving me a tour?" she asked lightly. "Or are you making an announcement?"

Harlan looked over at her and grinned. "It's a fine day for a walk, don't you think?"

She was laughing as he parked, though she couldn't have said why. But that giddy feeling didn't go anywhere as she climbed out of the truck and walked with him, from one end of the little slice of a mountain town to the other.

He greeted everyone they passed. He introduced her as his wife. And while his friends and neighbors were exclaiming over that surprise, he filled her in on who they all were and how they all related to each other, like one big Cowboy Point tree of many families.

"The Bennett sisters are newcomers," he told her when they passed by Mountain Mama, the pizza and ice cream place. The renovated barn was even more cheerful up close than it had seemed while driving by. Inside, everything was brightly painted to be as vibrant and inviting as possible and, she imagined, was a happy sort of beacon in the dark of winter. "They're from somewhere at lower elevation. Colorado maybe. Some folks come up here and try to open businesses that don't make a lot of sense and don't last through the first big snow. It looks like they knew what they were doing, because they've been here five years now and most nights, you have to wait to get a table. Even in winter."

"I guess the pizza must pretty good, then."

"They claim that it's a family recipe, handed down in secret through the generations," Harlan said with a grin. "Wilder claims it's crack. I don't know what it is, but it keeps us all coming back."

He nodded toward the wide lot next to the barn. "Folks are already clamoring for them to expand." Harlan lifted his chin in the direction of the store across the street but there was something... tighter in his features. "It's just about warm enough for the coffee cart. That's another newcomer and another new business, but it took off last summer. There's talk of getting something going year-round for that, too. Everyone likes coffee."

But Kendall was following his gaze to the General Store. "You don't like that place."

Harlan's mouth crooked. "It's not about liking it or not liking it. That General Store has been around since the first Copper Mountain miners figured out that first, there wasn't any copper, and second, it was exhausting to make that ten-mile trip up and down the mountain. If you ask the Lisles, the current owners, how the store came to be, they'll give you a song and dance about how Ebenezer Lisle settled the whole of Montana and half of America on his way here. Then, out of the goodness of his heart, set up an outpost to give back to his associates."

"Why do you sound personally offended by something that had to happen in... what?... the 1800s?"

"Not offended. But if you ask my family, or anyone who knows the actual history of Cowboy Point, the Careys were here first."

Kendall squinted up at him, looking at the laughter in his gaze but the stern set of his jaw. Like he thought this was silly... but also true. "I thought you were ranchers. All that land out there backs that up. What do you want with a store?"

Harlan shook his head at her sadly. "At first there was nothing here but a busted-up mine, and a questionable pack of miners milling around. Legend has it that there was a high-stakes poker game, and Ebenezer Lisle won the store from crusty old Matthew Carey with a royal flush. The Lisles claim it was down to good old-fashioned luck, a family gift, the way they tell it. But we know that the Lisles aren't lucky. They cheat."

Kendall stared at him in amazement. "And you're still arguing about this? Over a hundred years later?"

"Folks take claims mighty seriously in these parts," Harlan told her, all drawl and that gleam in his gaze. "And I wouldn't say that anyone's actively feuding these days, except maybe my brother Wilder and Tennessee Lisle, the way they have been since kindergarten. But no one's *forgotten*, either."

Kendall couldn't help but laugh at that. "This all sounds very healthy and not at all small town."

"This," Harlan said, almost gently, "is how the West was won, Kendall. One ancient blood feud and tall tale at a time."

And when she smiled, Harlan gazed down at her in that same intense way of his that made her feel even more shivery than usual, out here in the sunlight on a public road where anyone could see.

She felt her smile fade. But the more it did, the more his gaze seemed… brighter, somehow.

Until her heart was pounding so hard in her chest that

she didn't know what might happen next. Would she topple over? Would she topple... into him? Would she do what she really wanted to do and kiss this man, her husband, the way she'd longed to do when she'd had the chance at their wedding?

She was only aware that someone walked up to them because Harlan straightened. And then had his hand on her back in the kind of unconsciously chivalrous gesture that made her want to... melt, maybe.

All over him.

"You couldn't make it down the length of the street without the gossip beating you to the punch," said the man who stood there. He was another tall one, with broad shoulders and a star on his chest that read *Sheriff*. The name on the other side read *Wayne*. Kendall's first thought was *Batman?* "I hear congratulations are in order."

Harlan grinned. "This is my wife, Kendall." He looked down at her. "Kendall, this is Deputy Sheriff Atticus Wayne. He's the reason Cowboy Point is free of any latter-day gunslingers."

"We prefer to avoid high noon situations whenever possible," the deputy sheriff agreed.

And when he and Harlan got into a discussion about the details of the last town meeting, Kendall knew that really, she ought to pay attention. She knew she ought to study the things they were saying so that she could make a contribution, so she could make sure to earn her place in this partnership she and Harlan were meant to be building.

But her belly was full. She was drunk on all those family dynamics and the laughter that had been its soundtrack.

Then again, maybe it was the May sunshine. Or this place—this lovely, happy little wide part of a remote road, tucked away from the world. She would have said that Paradise Valley itself was off the beaten track.

But if that was the case, then Cowboy Point was trackless.

And yet, somehow, it didn't feel like she was *hiding* here.

She stood there on the main drag where everyone could see her, letting the sunlight dance all over her. When she looked around, she found herself waving at these people who were her neighbors now, who she could tell already knew who she was even if she hadn't met them.

Yet.

And the truth was that she couldn't wait to explore each and every one of these places. To meet the people that Harlan had told her stories about, and the ones she hadn't learned about yet. To settle into all of this, so that she, too, could be a story these folks told.

About the wife he'd brought home from somewhere else, a newcomer in one sense, but connected to him just the same. Almost as if she was as rooted here as deeply as his family was, by proxy, stretching all the way back to a disputed poker game that the participants' descendants were still pissed about.

Deep down, she felt a surge of something like anticipation, like she couldn't wait.

Like she already belonged here.

Like she was ready to spend a little quality time in a fairy tale.

Or, after so many years out there running from other people's bad decisions, like she was finally home.

Chapter Six

HARLAN LIKED BEING married.

Or he liked being married to Kendall, anyway.

May got brighter and warmer, then rolled over into June—which came in with a snowstorm like it was March again, because this was Montana. This high up in the mountains, summer was never a given no matter what it said on the calendar.

And Harlan found he could put up with the vagaries of the weather just fine when there was more daylight to go around. That was the point of June, to his mind, no matter if it was snowing or not. Happily, the snow didn't last. And even the chilliest pastures on the ranch warmed up again when there were fewer long shadows to keep the land cold.

With one thing and another, it was headed towards the middle of the month and the official start of summer before he knew it.

Meaning he'd been married more than a month. Almost two.

Once he'd decided to get married, and quick, he'd assured himself that it would work out no matter who answered his ad. Harlan figured that a marriage was like any other relationship and he had business relationships and friendships stretching back decades. He'd believed that he and whoever he married would settle into each other the way people had done throughout history when the marriage was when they'd gotten to know each other. He'd assumed that they would find a way to make things work, one way or another. That at the very least they'd set up a routine they could both depend on to make their days hum along well, because the partnership was the part of the marriage that mattered.

What he hadn't expected was that it would be so easy. Or feel so... effortless.

He looked forward to seeing her every morning. He rolled out of bed long before sunrise and got a first round of coffee going, so he could choke down a cup before he trudged out to do the morning round of chores. The same way he knew his dad had always done for both his mother and Belinda, and Lord knew, Zeke had always been a happily married man. By the time he got back, Kendall was up and showered, there was a fresh pot brewing, and she was setting out a hot breakfast.

It was amazing how cared for a man could feel with a hot meal in his belly on a cold morning.

Over breakfast, they worked out what their day would look like in consultation with the rest of the family in the group text, where all of his brothers checked in and they divided up the tasks. They decided what could be done individually or what required that they gather together to get something bigger handled. Sometimes it was a local ranch thing, sometimes it was Boone's dairy farm, sometimes it was all about the hay they sold to ranchers all over the West.

Kendall came with him some days, particularly when he knew he was headed out into some of the most beautiful and remote parts of the ranch. Other times, she stayed behind to handle the office—a job she'd volunteered for in her first week. Within the month she had not only familiarized herself with the mountains of paperwork that routinely gave him headaches, but had reorganized the room he used as an office and set up a system to handle things like invoices, vendors, and outstanding bills.

Harlan often thought he would have married her for that alone, had he had even the slightest inkling that the wife he'd decided to get could also be a kind of office manager, not only capable of handling the tasks that tied him in knots, but good at them.

More than that, she even seemed to *enjoy* doing that kind of stuff, which he found nothing short of miraculous.

Some days on the ranch called for all hands on deck, like the vaccinations and castrations of the season's calves. And if Harlan had expected Kendall to be squeamish about the necessities of ranch life—and the ranching business—he was in for a surprise. She took to it the way Belinda had back when she'd started coming around, elbows deep in what needed doing and no complaints.

"Seems like you got yourself a good one there," Wilder said that bright June day as he and Harlan took a breather after a particularly tough round of wrestling disobedient calves into the corral to get taken care of.

Harlan didn't have to look over at Kendall, who had been given instructions about what she needed to do to help and had nodded, then waded on in. She was as muddy as the rest of them now, which he viewed as a badge of honor.

The thing was, muddy on Kendall translated to cute.

Much too cute for a family day involving castrating the bull calves to make them steers—and notably less aggressive.

So cute it was hard to focus. He didn't want to give Wilder any encouragement, as part of his lifelong personal policy regarding handling his brothers, but he couldn't keep himself from grinning. "I can't complain."

"I heard a rumor," Wilder drawled, clearly encouraged. Harlan lost the grin. "The story is, Jack Stark dared you to put out an ad for a wife. And you, Harlan James Carey, known for taking exactly zero risks in the course of your lifetime, went ahead and took that dare."

Harlan stared at Wilder. Wilder smirked. "I'm just telling you what I heard."

"You didn't."

"Hear it? Pretty sure I did, brother. Loud and clear."

Harlan sighed. "You didn't hear a random rumor floating through the pines, Wilder. You were out carousing with the Starks and they shot their mouth off about what their cousin might or might not have done."

The way Wilder laughed, Harlan knew, was as good as an admission of guilt. Jack Stark, the oldest of all the Stark cousins in his generation, was a lot like Harlan. Steady. Determined. It was some of his younger cousins—Steven Stark's disreputable pack of wildcat sons, who'd grown up motherless and had basically lived by their wits and their willingness to throw down—who were the rowdy, rumor-mongering Starks.

The rest of the extended family were jack's younger sisters, dreamy Matilda who liked small, furry animals better than people and poor Rosie, who was a local scandal these days because she had twin toddlers—and refused to name their father no matter how many times her male relatives demanded she tell them so they could sort the man out. And, of course, there was Sarah Jane, Cowboy Point's librarian, who was the closest thing to a proper Old West schoolmarm Harlan had ever seen.

He knew exactly where Wilder had heard about his mail-order ad.

"So that's a yes or no on the newspaper ad campaign?" When Harlan only gazed back at him, sternly, Wilder laughed. "Maybe I want to follow your example. After all, Dad told all of us to get moving on the wife and kids front. Not surprising that you took that as seriously as you did. You always have been the most competitive."

"That would be you," Harlan said, shaking his head.

"You and Ryder, since the day you two were born."

"Before we were born, if the stories are true," Wilder said in lazy agreement, though his gaze was as intent as ever. "Dad always likes to say that we were wrestling in the womb."

Because only a fool thought Wilder was as lazy as he acted, Harlan continued, "I should have gotten married a long time ago. And I would have, but there always seemed to be too much to do around here to be bothered with finding the right woman."

His brother shook his head. For what seemed like an unnecessarily long time, to Harlan's mind.

"That's the saddest thing I've ever heard you say," Wilder said. Eventually. "I find the right woman every Friday and Saturday night. She's not the *same* right woman, mind you. But *right now* works just fine."

Harlan didn't dignify that with a response—because he knew his brother wanted one—and he felt especially virtuous when he didn't even roll his eyes. "I should have gotten it done years ago," he said again. "If I had, maybe there would already be grandkids running around the place. I know that's what he really wants."

And what he wouldn't get if his sons didn't get a move on—though Harlan didn't say that either. He didn't have to say it. None of them had said much about Zeke's diagnosis since he'd made his announcement, but then, none of them had to.

What was there to say about something so profoundly unimaginable?

Even Wilder had nothing smart-ass to say as they both looked over to where Zeke was sitting up on an ATV with Belinda at his side, the pair of them discussing something with great intensity—knowing his father and stepmother, it was likely what to have for dinner.

Over by the fence, Knox and Kendall were engaged in some kind of conversation that had Kendall looking fascinated in that way of hers, with a smile and her clever gaze so curious, while Knox laughed his head off as he told a story that involve a lot of hand gestures.

Both of those things—his father hale and hearty for the moment and his wife wrapped up in the middle of his family like this—and Harlan's ribs felt almost too tight to breathe.

"It doesn't seem real," Wilder said quietly, no longer sounding the slightest bit lazy. "That he can be sick."

"It doesn't," Harlan agreed in the same tone, and was grateful when Boone gave the sign to let the next set of calves through.

Because however little time his father had left, he was here now. That was what mattered.

That was what he held onto as the afternoon wore on and they all worked together, one big family missing only Ryder. Out on this land that had been in Carey hands for generations and would, God willing, stay in Carey hands for generations to come.

Out beneath that big Montana sky that felt like theirs and theirs alone on days like this.

He liked being married, he thought again, as he and Kendall headed back to his house when the day was done, both of them a little bit dirty and a whole lot tired. He liked not being on his own. He liked having her there beside him so they could talk about the day and share it all. Those tiny little moments, so easily forgotten, that stitched together and were the basis of everything. The point of it all.

Houses were built one brick at a time. Maybe what he was learning was that marriages were too.

"You never have told me why you moved around as much as you did," he said later that night.

They'd thrown together an easy dinner after such a long day. And there was more light in the sky now, it being June, so they took their food out to what he'd always considered the summer porch, where they could sit under the trees and enjoy being outside.

Harlan thought that life really couldn't get a whole lot better than it was in that moment.

He was so busy with that thought that it took him a minute to realize that she hadn't responded. When he looked over, Kendall seemed unduly preoccupied with her plate. And with the process of cutting herself a bite of the meat that he knew was tender enough to fall off the bone, because if a Carey knew anything in this world, it was meat.

"You really don't want to answer the question, do you?"

he asked, with a laugh.

Kendall put down her fork and knife without actually taking her next bite. She didn't look up at him.

"In your family everyone is welcoming, but not putting on some kind of act. They all seem generally themselves. It's lovely." She looked up then, a kind of set, nearly wary expression on her face that he'd never seen before. "That's not how everyone is, though. I'm not sure you know that. I'm not sure you understand how rare it is."

"I've met more than a few folks in my time who didn't exactly make honesty and transparency their watchword," he replied, not sure why he felt... stung. "Cowboy Point might seem like it's not a part of the world, because we like it that way, but it is."

"What you have here is rare," Kendall said, too quietly. "That's all I'm trying to say."

"I don't believe you're trying to say anything," he observed. And sure, he still felt that sting, but it was also true. "You're doing what you always do. You deflect. You change the subject so fast it's hard to remember there was ever a subject at all."

To her credit, she didn't look away. "Is that a problem for you?"

And it should have been. Harlan knew that. It should have been a big, bright red flag. A hard no.

He had always prided himself on honesty. He had always insisted on integrity, in himself and anyone close to him.

But this was Kendall. She was already his wife.

The real problem was that he knew he wasn't going anywhere.

"It's a problem," he told her, after a moment. "But not a dealbreaker."

She considered him. "How much of a problem are we talking about?"

Harlan studied her face in the light of the small lantern he'd set up in the center of the table, while the sky played with shades of blue far above. "I want to know who you are, Kendall. Is that a bad thing?"

"It's not you wanting to know me that's the bad thing. It's that I don't think you'll like what you find out."

He sat back in his chair, the pretty near-summer evening forgotten. "Are you a murderer?"

She let out a laugh, then swallowed it. "Um. No. What a question to ask."

"Are you wanted by the law in any capacity, in any state of this union or abroad?"

The startled laughter on her face faded. "No."

Something else occurred to him, and he wondered why he hadn't asked this before. "Are you already married to someone else?"

He watched color flood her face. "Absolutely not. I wouldn't—" But she cut herself off.

"Just trying to cover all the bases here," he said, with a shrug. "Trying to work out what's so terrible that you think if you tell me, I'll kick you off the mountain."

And he'd said that last park as a joke, really. Because of course he wouldn't be kicking anyone anywhere, but the moment he said it he could see that she thought that's exactly what might happen.

"Some people have a past," she told him, carefully. "It's not the kind of past you have, filled with tales of poker games, crusty old miners, and family legacies that come with an expansive and beautiful acreage. Some people's pasts are a bit darker than that. And significantly more distressing."

But he had married her on the same gut feeling that he had now. The same gut feeling that governed all the things he did, and if Harlan was wrong about her, he was wrong about everything. Absolutely everything.

He just didn't believe that was possible.

"I'm a man who makes up my own mind. Your past isn't going to sway me one way or another." He moved a hand to indicate both of them and the table between them. "This. Here. Now. That's what matters, Kendall. That's all that matters."

And the smile she aimed his way then was heartbreaking. "I hope so," she said softly. "I really do hope so."

She stood then, gathering up their plates to take them inside.

And he almost let it go.

Almost.

But when she came back out, Harlan stood and reached

out to put a hand on her arm when she drew near.

And it was like the summer night shimmered into stillness all around them. Like the earth beneath their feet came to a shuddering halt.

He forgot, completely, what he'd meant to do. Why he'd stood up in the first place.

Because the night was soft around them and her eyes gleamed green, like pine trees and the best part of summer. And that same spark was there between them, blooming brighter than any flower could have.

It was that humming thing in him, bursting into a full throated song.

Because his hand was on her arm, his palm flush against the soft skin of her bicep, and he could feel that touch in every part of his body. He could feel the intensity of that connection, like she was hardwired into him, so that even so simple a touch was like flipping a switch.

He'd spent all these weeks pretending, he realized then.

Pretending he didn't dream about her at night. Pretending he wasn't consumed, that he wasn't obsessed. Looking for excuses to touch her whenever he could, so he could hoard them up and go over them like polished coins, one after the next, when he was alone.

She was a fever in his blood, and God help him, but he liked the burn.

And now, here, everything seemed possible.

More than possible.

He dropped his gaze to that mouth of hers that had captivated him from the start. Tonight it looked vulnerable, sensual.

And he wanted more. He wanted her to brush her lips over his again, but more than that, he wanted her to follow that up. To kiss him like she meant it. To move closer, put her hands on him, and then indulge herself in him the way he dreamed of indulging himself in her.

"Kendall," he managed to grate out. "I want to kiss you more than I want to take my next breath."

Her eyes widened at that. Her lips parted, just slightly. Just enough to make his obsession all the worse. He watched something shiver over her, and through her as she blew out a breath.

"That sounds like a serious condition," she said, what seemed like an eternity later. And her eyes were a dark green now, like she was part of the pines rising all around them. "I wouldn't want you to pass out from a lack of breathing, Harlan. I think you'd better kiss me."

And so he did.

At last, he did.

Something roared in him, deep and resolutely male in a way he did not usually allow himself to indulge. He pulled her closer, careful but sure, and he slid his hands up to take her face between them.

Then, finally, he leaned down and fit his mouth to hers.

And everything became that same song.

It rose in him like a whole chorus, singing loud.

He angled his head so he could take more of her, learning the way she kissed and teaching her what he liked. It was a tangle of tongues and a dance, a perfect dance to all that wild and perfect singing, as they found their rhythm.

As the heat between them blazed hot.

As the need for her thudded in him, the irresistible drumbeat more intense with every second.

He wanted to get closer. He wanted to kiss her forever, and he wanted *more*.

Harlan wanted everything.

There was no pretending, now, that he was anything but infatuated with this woman. *Fascinated* didn't begin to cover it.

It didn't help that she tasted better than she looked. That the particular chemistry of his mouth and hers was something several degrees more than extraordinary—

Maybe she knew it too, because she wrenched her mouth away from his then.

And for a moment they were breathing together, stricken in the same way. He could tell. She had the same astonished look on her face that he felt in him.

Everywhere in him.

"Kendall..." he began, though he didn't recognize his own voice.

Her hands had made their way to his chest and she pushed herself back to look up at him. With eyes so dark, now, that he couldn't see any green at all.

"You like making a mess, don't you," Kendall said.

Harlan made himself step back. He ran a hand over his face. "What?"

"This is what you do." Her voice was calm, but her gaze was nothing short of hectic. "You like to drop a bomb, then sit back and wait to see what happens. Isn't that what you did when you threw me like a grenade into the middle of your family's Sunday dinner?"

"I don't think I like the way you're categorizing that."

"You say you want to know about me." She moved away from him, putting more space between them. "Do you really? Or is it all a stockpile of weapons you like to gather, then seek to deploy when it suits you best?"

"It was a kiss, Kendall."

And he was surprised to find that he was actually getting a little hot as he stood there. When he would have said that he'd gotten rid of his own temper a lifetime ago. Because there had never been any point to it.

He'd been angry when his mother died. He'd been angry when his father remarried, and angrier still that he couldn't hate Belinda the way he'd wanted to. He'd been angry that the twins were so disruptive, but so funny. Angrier still that Boone and Knox insisted on being impossible to dislike.

He'd been sixteen and like many sixteen-year-old young men, he'd been *angry*.

So he'd poured it into football. Then he'd taken all that

temper, all of that heat, and sunk deep inside of him until he'd given it to the land.

And now everything that mattered in him was the ranch, so nothing in him was personal.

Except this.

Except Kendall, who was looking at him as if she knew exactly where his temper was and was poking at it deliberately.

"You're so interested in knowing what my life is like," she was saying. "I'll tell you that one thing I got very good at, out there, was reading people. Especially men. Everyone thinks that they're great at hiding their feelings when the truth is, few people really are. You took pleasure in causing a commotion that night, Harlan. Why?"

He couldn't understand why this was what she wanted to talk about. Right at this moment. When he could still taste her in his mouth.

"I don't know," he bit out, amazed that he could also taste his own temper. Like Kendall was the one person alive who could access even the parts of him he'd been certain he'd laid to rest a lifetime back.

And now she was looking at him like she could see straight through him. "I don't believe you."

Harlan shook his head, trying to get a handle on all the things surging in him now. "Look, I'm not the kind of man who goes around hating his life, going through the motions, wishing for things he can't have. I like who I am. I like what

I do. I wouldn't do it if I didn't." He ran a hand over his face once again, but that felt like he was fidgeting when he had never been the kind of man who *fidgeted*, so he dropped it to his side. "But that doesn't mean that every now and again, I don't think about what it might be like to shake up everyone's ideas about who I am. To remind them that I'm not actually one of the mountains around here. That I can be as surprising as anyone else. Sometimes they forget that I'm methodical and dependable because I choose to be, not because I can't be just as spontaneous as anyone else."

She was breathing too hard, he thought. Too heavily for the circumstances—or maybe she was having trouble handling the way that same song was swelling in him still. Maybe it was in her, too.

"Thank you," Kendall said quietly. "I can tell that was honest."

"Maybe you can tell me something in return. Why would you want to talk about that Sunday dinner with my family now. Now, of all times?"

"Because," she threw at him, fiercely. *Desperately*, something in him whispered. "I don't want to be a mess you make, Harlan. My life is messy enough on its own. This is supposed to be an escape."

"From what?" And he was aware of the urgency in his voice, though there was nothing he could do about it.

Just like there was nothing he could do to keep his fingers from twitching with the urge to get his hands on her once more, though he kept them to himself.

Somehow, he kept them to himself.

Yet she didn't answer him either way. She held his gaze for what felt like an eternity, and then she turned and left him there.

Standing out beneath the June sky as it slowly, slowly darkened. With all that heat still inside him, and that song as loud as ever.

But he had a clear understanding that he couldn't go after her. Not now. Not like this, when she didn't trust him.

No matter how much he thought they both wanted him to.

Chapter Seven

THAT KISS KEPT her up all night.

She tossed and turned and *yearned* for things she couldn't name—and things she definitely could—until the hours were less wee and more like morning. When she woke at her usual time she was out of sorts. Her eyes were swollen. She felt cranky and upset and was absolutely certain that she was going to come out of her bedroom to find Harlan waiting for her, so he could deliver an order for her to pack up and get out.

Kendall accepted in that moment, rubbing at her eyes in her bedroom before facing the fallout of the night before, that she didn't want to go. She didn't want to leave this place, these people.

But most of all, she really didn't want to leave Harlan.

It was absurdly hard to make herself stand up and leave that room, then walk through this house she'd come to like so much. She had to *force* herself to go into the kitchen.

Harlan was waiting for her. Kendall had known he would be waiting for her, and she braced herself—

But he didn't say anything. He took a long look at her. Then he prepared her a mug of coffee the way she liked it, sweeter and lighter than she ought to take it, but life was short. And usually unpleasant, so why make it more so? That was what she liked to tell herself.

Today she didn't tell herself anything. She watched as he stirred the concoction just the way she did, the spoon making a metallic clink against the side of the ceramic mug.

When he handed it to her she took it. She cradled it between her hands, took the first glorious sip, and didn't look at him while she did it.

Maybe she was just girding her loins.

"I'm sorry if I upset you last night," he said.

Straight out.

Because that was Harlan, she understood then, as her gaze snapped to his. Straight and to the point. He didn't hide from anything, not even apologizing.

He'd been showing her this all along but somehow, she hadn't imagined it would extend to an actual apology. Kendall couldn't remember the last time someone had apologized to her. Much less sincerely.

But she could see the intensity in his gaze. There was no doubt at all that he meant it.

"I'm sorry too," she said, past the lump in her throat and that strange, fluttering sort of feeling that seemed to swamp her where she stood. "It's possible I flew off the handle a little more than necessary."

What struck her most was how hard that was to say to him.

Almost as if she'd gotten used to being in the right by default, because where her family was concerned, that was a given. And it turned out that she didn't like admitting any sort of fault at all—and wasn't *that* a wake-up call?

"I think," she clarified, because she didn't want to be the kind of person who *couldn't* apologize, having lived with two of them her whole life, "that what I mean is, I did do that. I did go overboard. And I'm sorry."

"You can take as much time as you want to come around the idea of getting physical with me, Kendall," he said, and she froze, her coffee mug halfway to her mouth. Because he was looking straight at her, and his dark eyes on her like that made her feel something a whole lot like giddy. "Maybe you'll never get there, and that will mean we'll have a different conversation down the line. But I want to be clear that as happy as I am to wait for you to be comfortable, I want you."

He said that the same way he'd apologized. Straight out. No *I think* or *maybe*. Just a statement of fact.

It made her whole body flush, red and hot.

Everywhere.

And he knew it. He could see it. She could tell.

"I've wanted you since the moment I laid eyes on you," he said then, only the touch of more gravel in his voice letting her know this conversation was getting to him, too. That it wasn't just her. "You living here, sharing the house with me and sharing this life with me, is making it a pretty constant desire on my part. You don't have to do anything about that. I'm not trying to put pressure on you. But I don't want there to be any confusion."

Kendall wanted to tell him that she felt a lot of things right then, but *confusion* wasn't one of them. Yet she couldn't manage to make her mouth work. She couldn't get any words out.

There was only that heat inside her, burning her alive.

"I'm not trying to make a mess," Harlan said in that impossibly low voice of his, like smoke and velvet. "But I do, very much, want to get you naked and stay that way a while."

Her lips moved but still, no words came out. Kendall could only stare back at him, stricken. And, she could admit, elated.

That was the only word for it. She was flooded with delight, and too many images to make sense of.

Harlan watched her for a long moment and she thought she saw the corner of his mouth crook, just the slightest bit. "Okay, then. Clarity achieved."

He said no more about it. But then, he didn't have to.

It was the fact of this attraction, that he didn't hide from it or disguise it. The fact that he wanted her and wasn't afraid to say it. The more interesting fact that *she* wanted *him* just the same, in a way she had never wanted anyone. So much that it scared her, a little.

Because she didn't know how it was possible to want anyone like that and not have it used against her. Eventually. Because as she knew all too well, anything and everything could be weaponized, and especially emotions.

Harlan went about his usual work that day, leaving Kendall to settle into the office. She did, but it was hard to concentrate, when she usually loved the cool embrace of numbers and bills and questions that had only one answer. She was too busy thinking that for all intents and purposes, that had been their first fight. And in her experience, even if a person *said* that things were fine or smoothed things over, a fight never really ended. It was never *really* resolved. It kept coming around, taking on new forms, and resurrecting itself at the slightest provocation.

But as day after day passed, it began to occur to her that Harlan… really was a man who meant what he said. That every now and again he liked to be spontaneous and he enjoyed the fallout from that when he did it. He'd admitted that.

Other than those occasions, he was a *what you see is what you get* kind of a man. The *salt of the earth, man of his word,* honest and downright *good* man she'd always believed was a fairy tale.

Kendall did not doubt that he wanted her the way he said he did.

But he didn't push that. He didn't grab her or even look at her in a way that made her uncomfortable. It was more like his confession had lit a match, and now that flickering flame ran through everything.

That spark. That heat.

One night she stopped in the door to the living room on her way to bed. Harlan was sitting in the chair he liked best, his feet up and a book on his lap with that long dusk outside and the mountains peering in. He looked beautiful, she thought. Just... *beautiful.*

Like the kind of man she'd never believed could truly exist.

That hot... but he liked to read? That implacably gorgeous... but not full of himself?

He was a unicorn, she thought, and since when did a Darlington happen across magic like this?

That she would ruin this was certain. She was genetically predisposed to destroy anything she touched.

Still, she was speaking before she could think better of it. "You never asked if I want you too."

He looked up and fixed her with the sort of look that was patient, hot, and entirely too knowing for her peace of mind.

"I don't need you to tell me, Kendall. I know that you do." His dark eyes gleamed. "I can see it all over you."

That night, she lay in her bed, wide awake. She tossed and turned, awash in a feeling of sheer disbelief—though it was edged out, as the hours ticked by, with irritation instead. Mostly at herself, but she aimed some at him, too.

If Harlan was trying to get under her skin, it was working.

But it was full-on summer now, so Montana was getting to her too. The mountains were covered in wildflowers, carpeting everything in bright colors beneath the endlessly blue sky. The evenings were light until late and it was like everyone had the same kind of summer fever. Because after the winter's cold and dark, for months and months, if the weather was nice, Montanans were going to take advantage of it.

Cowboy Point was nothing short of vibrant come July, to better take advantage of as many light-filled, graceful summer hours as possible.

There was a weekly Farm and Craft Market. Produce and food stands appeared at the foot of every dirt road. The Art Collective, a community of artistic types that lived a ways out in hills, had a pop-up gallery in one of the fields along the main road in fine weather. There were alpaca ranchers turned fiber enthusiasts, artisan dyers, and yarn stockists out of one of the buildings on the main street. Mountain Mama Pizza had live music out on their patio, and the General Store set up picnic tables out front while their connected diner ran summer plate specials, all from locally sourced ingredients.

In the long evenings, when it seemed as if the sun couldn't quite make up its mind whether or not to sink behind the mountains, the community gathered in all of these places and over at the Copper Mine, the bar across the creek. They too put out picnic tables in the field next to it and strung up lights that reached nearly all the way to the church and its Thursday pancake suppers. Most nights the bar also had locals come in with food trucks to help celebrate the joy of these summer nights.

"I'm not much for nightlife," Harlan told her in the beginning of the real summer in July. "But I've also lived here since birth. I have community whether I want it or not. I don't want *you* to feel isolated."

And so this husband of hers who made it clear he wanted her, but never pushed that boundary, took her out almost every night. He made sure she couldn't help but meet the people who were the fabric that made up Cowboy Point. The families that had been here forever. The newcomers who'd maybe only been here a generation or two, instead of three or four. The folks who were truly brand new, who might or might not stick it out through winter.

Locals took bets on that, she discovered. There was a book on it in the General Store.

But the people Kendall found she liked to pay the most attention to were Harlan's brothers. Her brothers too, now, she supposed, though it felt funny to think about the Careys as *family*. *Her* family, no less. Particularly when to them, *family* wasn't a dirty word.

"It's like watching a television show," she told Harlan one night, sitting next to him on a picnic bench out behind the Copper Mine. The creek looked inviting, this side of a nice and hot July day. It tended to cool down at night, this high up, but she liked that, too. She'd spent too many summers in much hotter places and had never enjoyed the feeling of incinerating the moment she stepped outside. She was a little suspicious of those who did. "Your brothers are like local gods."

"Everyone's a local god in a place this small," Harlan replied. "We all end up in the community tabloids sooner or later. It's just that the tabloids here are the stories everyone tells each other. My brothers star in a lot of those stories because they're single."

"But they're all a different kind of single." Kendall leaned closer to Harlan, so she could speak directly into his ear. She nodded toward Wilder, because it was always fun to look around at all the women who were making eyes at him—or trying not to seem as if they were making eyes at him. "I'm trying to guess which of the ladies staring at him have actually been with him and which ones just consider him aspirational."

"I don't want to know," Harlan muttered, but Kendall could tell that he did.

"No spoilers," she cautioned him. "I want to see how it plays out."

She moved her attention over to Boone, who never made as much of a scene as the others. Possibly because he was often in the company of his best friend, a local girl who was married to someone else who was never with her. But what Kendall noticed was that even when his best friend wasn't around, Boone didn't seem to see another woman. No matter how many of them mooned around in his direction.

"Boone and Sierra have been best friends since they were kids," Harlan told her when she mentioned this. "She used to run around with him all over the ranch."

That was hard to imagine, Kendall thought, then thought better of saying. Because every time she saw Sierra, the woman looked... weighed down. Maybe even sad, especially when Boone wasn't making her laugh.

Another thing she kept to herself was the fact that in her experience, men and women being *best friends* wasn't really a thing. Usually, one of them was nursing deeper feelings—or an attraction they could only deal with by spending all that time together and pretending not to feel what they felt.

And the thing about that kind of dynamic was that it always blew up. Eventually.

Kendall knew better than to say all of that, even to Harlan. Because, in her experience, men did not read these undercurrents the way women did.

The antidote to all of that being Knox, who acted as if he had a spotlight attached to him at all times. As if he was forever on the stage—and in the center of that stage. Something he was clearly more than okay with.

"Really," Kendall said into Harlan's ear, "they're all ridiculously entertaining."

Another man might have questioned her interest in his brothers, but not Harlan. Because Harlan looked at her with that dark gaze of his and Kendall just... melted. No matter how cool the summer night was at this elevation.

Harlan, she knew, was not concerned about who Kendall was looking at.

"Wait until you meet Ryder," he told her, toying with his beer bottle on the table in front of him like that might distract them both from the fact that she was sitting so close to him that her leg was flush against his. "He's actually an entertainer by trade. If you can call the rodeo entertaining."

Kendall pretended her pulse wasn't rocketing around inside her. "You don't like the rodeo? What kind of cowboy are you?"

"The kind who works for a living," Harlan replied with a drawl. "No applause necessary."

Some nights they danced to the music at Mountain Mama, out on that patio. Harlan took her in his arms and whirled her around and around until she wasn't sure she was dizzy from the way they moved or just giddy, inside and out, because of him.

And then, every night, they would drive home with so many stars in the sky above them, that she felt like a mess either way. As if there was no hope for her but to surrender, completely.

Every summer night she thought she was that much closer to letting go for good.

And every summer morning, she woke up and thought that this life she'd stumbled into was as close to a charmed life as she'd ever had or ever would.

The trouble with that was, Kendall knew better than to believe in anything that felt charmed. That was a good way to make certain that the other shoe—because there was always another shoe and well did she know it—would drop right on her head.

But the July days seemed endlessly blue, bright and golden and sweet. One morning, Kendall drove down to the main house in the hardy old hatchback of indeterminate age that Harlan had told her was hers to use as she pleased. Like his truck, it ran better than some finer, newer cars she'd been in over the past five years.

The car was one more way he made her feel taken care of, but thinking too much about that was dangerous. It made her want to turn the car around and go find him, out there in the rolling hills of the ranch. And maybe do something about all the stars in a mess inside her that he'd put there himself.

But she didn't. She was running down to the General Store and she'd taken up the habit of dropping in to see if Belinda needed anything. It didn't take a lot to show someone consideration, she'd discovered. It didn't take turning herself inside out and scraping herself raw against another person's indifference. That was what *her* family demanded of her.

In *this* family, there might be a lot of teasing. The brothers like to jostle each other, with words as well as an unexpected shoulder, whenever possible. They were all particularly careful around Zeke, but she got the impression that was a new development. And it was obvious that underlying all of it was affection. What seemed like a genuine delight in each other's company.

And love.

That word she'd spent so much of her adult life trying to avoid. Because talking about love was depressing when you were a Darlington. Talking about love as a Darlington was like chatting intently about desert vacations when you were a fish.

Kendall liked coming to the main house on her own. There was a no-knock policy, so she let herself in. And without Harlan she could linger in the front hall, looking at the pictures of him from when he was small.

She had never felt anything quite like the sensations that moved through her when she stood there, looking at his past and wondering if that might really be her future, too—but she shook it off. She reminded herself that this was still temporary even when it felt like it wasn't.

Especially when it felt like it wasn't.

She headed toward the back of the house and could see Belinda out through the glass windows, moving around in her garden. But Zeke was in the kitchen and she stopped, surprised to find him standing there over what looked like a whole tabletop of... spurs. Gleaming ones. Embossed ones. Spurs featuring different metals and finishes.

"That's a lot of spurs," she said, perhaps obviously.

Zeke cracked a smile in her direction in a way that made her heart hurt, because Harlan was so much like him. "Some might say too many spurs," he drawled, with a glance out the windows toward his wife.

Kendall drew closer to the table and reached out a finger toward one of the shiny pairs, though she didn't touch the glossy surface. "These are so... pretty? I guess I've never thought of spurs as *pretty* before."

The back door opened and Belinda came in with a basketful of vegetable and greens. "You want some of those things?" she asked as she took in Kendall's interest in the spurs. "Please. We have too many."

"I'm not as spry as I used to be," Zeke said, with what had to be the world's best example of understatement, but who was Kendall to call him on it? "I can't be out there, mending fences day and night. And you know what they say about idle hands."

"He makes his own spurs. And bits." Belinda set her basket down on the counter with a thump. "And what are we supposed to do with a house full of spurs and bits, I ask you?"

Kendall blinked, and didn't think. "Bespoke cowboy accessories? You should sell them."

It took her a moment to realize that both Belinda and Zeke were frowning at her. She straightened from the table, sure that she'd overstepped.

"You mean one of those online things," Zeke said, and though that was a statement, Kendall heard it as more of a question.

Or she chose to answer it, anyway. "Sure, I bet you could sell them online. But you could also sell them at the Farm and Craft Market. I keep inventing reasons to go down there every week. There are so many cute little booths with unusual, unique things. I was talking to the organizer last week and she said that they get more and more tourists coming up from Marietta all the time, just to see the market and wander around Cowboy Point. What's a better souvenir than something handmade by a real cowboy?"

Zeke was already shaking his head. "Never have been much of a salesman. I can sell a man a bale of hay, but let's be honest. The hay sells itself."

"I wish I had all that time to sit around in a booth hoping tourists from Marietta happen by," Belinda said with a sniff.

And once again, Kendall didn't even consider what she was doing. She was talking before she knew she might open her mouth, almost like she was comfortable here. Almost like she believed in this charmed life and her place in it. "I can do it."

Once again, her in-laws stared at her.

And as they kept staring at her, she felt a deep compulsion to prove herself. She told herself it was healthy. Who wouldn't want to impress her mother- and father-in-law? It was a perfectly reasonable urge and had nothing to do with what she'd seen on a social media post regarding *attachment issues*.

"I'm actually pretty good at selling things," she told them, which was true. She did not intend to elaborate on the sort of things she sold. Given that most of the time, what she was selling was a particular narrative to explain terrible behavior away. Then again, wasn't all sales about storytelling? "I can be pretty persuasive, though I have to say, I don't think these will require I do much besides display them."

"It's your funeral," Belinda said, because Belinda was always the worst-case scenario person. Which was funny, because she was also the first person to laugh, or leap into the middle of an argument, or hell, start one. She was all about following her feelings, all the time.

Kendall found that admirable. And also intimidating.

But that was how she found herself driving down to the store with a selection of spurs and bits in a box beside her. She stopped in front of the General Store, but she took the box across the street instead so she could walk that little way down the road to the Mountain Mama barn.

And also so she could enjoy the fact that people waved at her, now. Like she really was one of them.

That made her feel ridiculously happy, so she was grinning as she went into the pizza place. It was doing a brisk business already though it wasn't yet noon. Kendall waited by the counter, still reveling in the fact that she already felt like a part of things. That she got to imagine that she *could be* a part of all this. She could identify most of the families seated at the tables inside the building and spilling out onto the patio. She knew the Bennett sisters, who owned and ran the place. She'd had several conversations with all three of them, all together and alone.

But she waited until she saw Flannery, the middle Bennett sister, come barreling out of the kitchen with her red hair in thick braids wrapped around her head, wearing an apron covered in flour. She smiled wide when she saw Kendall, but kept going, carrying the two pizzas she had in her hands out towards the waiting tables. When she came back, she was wiping her hands on her apron.

"Did you call in an order?" she asked.

"Actually, I'm hoping you have a second to talk about the Farm and Craft market," Kendall said. Flannery brightened and nodded, so Kendall explained Zeke's hobby. She set the box on the wide counter and opened it so Flannery could look at the spurs and the bits nestled inside. "What do you think? Is it worth setting up a booth?"

"Is it worth more local, bespoke art?" Flannery laughed. "Of course it is. This is exactly the kind of thing people are looking for. Come on down next Saturday and we'll get you all set up."

"That's it?" Kendall laughed. "I thought there'd be... I don't know, a whole process to go through."

"I aspire to a process," Flannery replied with a laugh. "If

I had my way, there would be so many people jostling for a booth that it would take an application process, a panel of judges, and a waiting list, but we're not there yet." She ran a finger down along the curve of one of the spurs. "I think this kind of thing is a step in that direction, though. Tell Zeke he's going to be the star of the market."

Kendall practically skipped back to the car, already thinking about ways that she could dress up a booth. She would have to ask the artist himself about a logo, and who knew? Maybe there should be a clever name to go along with it. Something that indicated Zeke's essential cowboyness, yet allowed the weekend warriors to dream about their own home on the ranges someday.

Inside the General Store, she behaved the way she always did when faced with the Lisle family. She acted as if no one had told her that there was the feud. She chatted with Cat, the younger Lisle sister who was usually behind the counter with her mother. She gave a wide berth to Cat's older brothers, who always looked at her as if she'd been sent in to spy on the place by Harlan.

As if it would be worth spying on a country store in the first place, and especially when all she needed were a few ingredients.

"I was talking to Flannery about a new booth at the Saturday market," she told Cat, because what she'd learned was that small-town people *chatted*. And the weirdest part was, Kendall liked the chatter. She wasn't playing along, she actually liked someone to say a pleasant hello to her when she entered a place. She very much liked it when the small talk was happy, funny, and made the process of buying anything and everything, that much more pleasant. There was a lot of that at the Farm and Craft market.

Kendall was looking forward to it. She wanted to see if she was as good at it as she thought she was.

Cat, who was the kind of beautiful, offhanded and effortless, that would send Kendall's mother and sister into a fury, sighed. "I keep telling my brothers that we should open a little booth at the market. But they don't see the point of having two stores open at the same time, and they outvote me."

She showed what she thought of family politics with a roll of her eyes, and Kendall laughed. And on her way outside, she stopped by the coffee truck that was parked outside the General Store now that it was summer, just as Harlan had promised. Inside, the lovely if mysterious Helena was pulling shots and foaming milk, and grinned when she saw Kendall. "A mocha again?"

Kendall liked that, too. She liked that it was known, what drink she'd prefer. That she was enough of a presence in this place that her drink order mattered.

"Yes," she said, smiling at Helena. "Thank you. And feel free to use a heavy hand on the chocolate."

Cowboy Point was beginning to feel like its own starry sky at her. A great big mess of people and places, and all of it beautiful. All of it meaningful in a way she never could have imagined before.

"Everyone here is so *invested*," she said that night, sitting out beneath the summer sky with Harlan. And it was a joy, she found, to sit with this man and ask him how his day had gone. To tell him about hers. It was such a simple, unexpected, pervasive joy. "They care about every piece of what they do. In the pizza place, every ingredient is as locally sourced as possible and they put those pizzas together with deliberate care, so that they're works of edible art. I know you don't like the General Store, but they *could* mark up their prices because they know that they have a captive audience since folks don't want to drive all the way down to Marietta for every little thing. But they don't."

Harlan shook his head. "I never thought I'd see the day when the Lisles are praised under my roof."

"We're outside." She laughed at the way he looked at her. "I've never lived in a place like this before. It's exciting to be around people who actually love to do what they do." Kendall leaned forward, cupping her chin in her hand. "You and your brothers love this land. It matters to you. I think that's what I'm trying to say. This is the place where things *matter*. I feel like somewhere along the way, people have lost that. It's a shame."

He didn't speak for a moment and the longer that went on, the more she began to notice the way he was looking at her. That crook in the corner of his mouth. The fact that

MEGAN CRANE

they had taken to sitting next to each other instead of across the table from each other. She didn't know when that had happened, when they had started inching closer and closer.

But when he reached out, she didn't pull away.

Instead, she sat so still that she could barely tell she was breathing. And Harlan took a piece of her dark hair that must have fallen down from her ponytail and carefully, tenderly, tucked it behind her ear.

Then smiled as goose bumps shimmered down her neck.

"We're all we've got," he said and it took a minute to remember what conversation they had been having. "If we don't care about this place or what we do, who will? It seems like every year there are more people who want to be here and fewer people acting like they were cursed because they were born here. It's a nice shift."

She was still trying to fight off the shivers. "Harlan…"

His haze grew more intense. More heated. "You want to be careful how you say my name," he told her, his voice quiet. "I don't want to misread the situation."

That was the trouble. He wasn't misreading anything. Kendall wanted to take that hand, bring it back, and maybe nestle her cheek into it while she was at it. She wanted to kiss him again, heedlessly. Recklessly.

But something in her balked when she thought about what would come after.

Because somewhere inside of her, she'd drawn that line. She couldn't continue to tell herself that it was temporary if she slept with him. She knew herself better than that. It was already hard as it was to keep herself from all the things she wanted.

Besides, a more cynical voice inside her chimed in, *the more intimacy you give him, the more ways he can disappoint you.*

Though she couldn't think of a single thing about him that could possibly be disappointing.

"That's what I thought," he said.

And then, the way he always did, he settled back into the evening as if nothing was tight or hot or *needy* there between them. As if he didn't feel that same spark that burned higher and higher in her by the day.

As if he was perfectly fine, leaving that fire to rage unchecked like that.

While *she* was quietly going out of her mind.

A few days later, after yet another restless night of dreams that were far too realistic and that made her much too sad to wake up from, she drove down from Cowboy Point into Marietta. She'd collected shopping lists from the whole family once they heard she was headed down the hill, and she wondered what it said about her that she truly liked the fact that they felt comfortable asking her. That they trusted her enough to do it.

Maybe that wasn't a big deal to some people, handing off a grocery list.

But to Kendall it felt like being accepted into the family.

Maybe, she thought as she navigated the winding road down Copper Mountain, what she really needed to think about was why the bar was always so low. Well, not *why*. She knew *why*. What she didn't know was why she was always *so surprised* every time her own alien upbringing was pointed out to her.

Because well-adjusted people not only didn't go and marry strangers, they certainly didn't think that a *shopping list* was anything more than that. A list. Of items to pick up from a grocery store. A thing that many people in bigger cities outsourced to complete strangers who operated delivery services.

She shook her head over that for most of those ten miles down Desolation Drive that she wasn't sure she'd ever really get used to. It was so *steep*. So relentlessly treacherous, even this close to August without a trace of snow or ice to be seen.

When she got to the bottom and drove into Marietta proper, she hunted down each and every item on every list in her hand. Because there was no point allowing her childhood trauma to make her a perfectionist in the strangest arenas unless she committed to it wholeheartedly, was there? She packed it all into bags and arranged them in her car, even taking the time to write each household's name on the bags that were theirs. Boone. Wilder. Knox. Main House.

But the best were the bags that said *ours*.

Hers and Harlan's. Like they really were a team. A unit.

Her last stop was the little pharmacy in town to pick up

something for Belinda. She parked on the street, finding Marietta prettier and more welcoming each time she came. Almost as if she was the one who was changing—becoming more and more like the sort of person who deserved that fairy-tale postcard life.

Though she knew better than to let herself get carried away. That was a road that couldn't possibly lead anywhere safe.

Inside, she waited in line and studied last year's Woman of the Year award that was displayed proudly behind the counter. She picked up Belinda's order, smiling to herself at the strident conversation the woman behind the counter— presumably said woman of yesteryear—was having with another townsperson, barely looking up at Kendall while she did it.

Not that Kendall minded. She found that she, too, wanted to know what the mayor was up to. In fact, she was filled with glee as she imagined asking people what they thought about the mayor of Marietta and her apparently filthy-rich husband up at the market this weekend.

What could be more delightfully small town than that?

Admit it, she told herself happily as she walked back outside. *This is beginning to feel like home.*

It was a beautiful day, clear and gorgeous. And sweet, bustling Marietta was a fine town. A wonderful place to visit. Kendall just couldn't help thinking that she liked Cowboy Point more. The tall pines. The kick of that high mountain air. The ranch that rolled on forever.

Harlan, she thought, or maybe something in her sang his name, these days.

Filled with all of that summer sweetness, she looked ahead to her car.

And stopped dead.

Right there in the middle of the sidewalk.

She felt, very distinctly, everything inside of her shatter, like she'd been glass all along and someone had just slammed a steel-toed boot straight through her gut.

It was so *sunny*. That was what seemed so wrong, suddenly. The sky was so blue and everything around her was pretty. Marietta was sparkling like a postcard, but Kendall could see the rot in it now.

She should have known better than to imagine it would ever go away.

Because it never did. That rot followed her around and here it was again, leaning up against her car. One of them had her head tipped back to take in the sun, the other was staring straight ahead at Kendall with a vindictive look on her face.

As always.

"Come on now, Kendall," Mayrose said in that sugar-wouldn't-melt voice of hers that felt like a kick in the stomach. And was meant to, she was well aware. "You didn't *really* think you could hide from us forever, did you?"

Next to her, Breanna stopped her sunbathing and focused on Kendall too, sweeping her hair back from her face and securing it on the top of her head with her sunglasses.

"Once a Darlington, always a Darlington, big sister," she said, with a drawl like honey and pure poison in her gaze. "When are you going to accept who you really are?"

And the way she laughed at that made everything inside Kendall run cold.

Because this was the other shoe she'd been afraid would fall on her all this time.

And here it was, landing on her head on a Marietta street and squashing her flat.

Chapter Eight

HARLAN HEARD ABOUT the altercation before Kendall made it back up Copper Mountain.

One of the Stark cousins was down in Marietta doing his own errands that day, and he'd called to let Harlan know that he had seen an interaction he didn't like much between Kendall and two strangers, right there on the street.

I don't want to go telling any stories, Logan Stark told him, a laughable claim under any other circumstances, as the Starks lived on stories like everyone else on their side of the mountain. *But the two strangers in question sure looked a lot like her.*

Harlan thanked him, asked after the current state of the Lodge restoration project to be neighborly, and spent the rest of his afternoon out feeding the cows and puzzling over the scene that Logan had described.

It was hard to imagine Kendall actually getting worked up about something. About anything. Logan had said he'd heard her with her voice raised, something Harlan couldn't imagine when she was always so steady. So quiet and watchful. Careful, even.

As if she was waiting, always waiting, to see which way

the wind would blow at any moment.

Maybe this was the wind she'd been waiting on.

Harlan couldn't wait to see if it had messed her up some, the way he'd like to do.

So much that he spent most nights enjoying a frigidly cold shower and didn't bother pretending it was for the health benefits. It wasn't. It was so he could keep his promises to Kendall and his hands to himself.

When he got back to the house, he expected her to come right out and tell him what happened, the way she did when new things happened around here. When she'd seen the group of dancers who were loosely connected to the art collective out beyond the ranch come into Cowboy Point and dance for the solstice. The way she had when she'd seen the signs for the upcoming Copper Mountain Rodeo in September and had wondered if she'd get to meet Ryder. The way she had when she'd seen him and his brothers round up the cattle on horseback.

Tonight she didn't come out to greet him in the foyer, wide-eyed and filled with stories. She sang out a hello from the kitchen, the sort he'd expect if nothing out of the ordinary had happened to her in the course of the day, so he thought on that while he went about his usual ritual of cleaning himself up from a day of hard labor before he went to find her.

When he got to the kitchen, showered so that he didn't smell like his work, she was focusing ferociously on food preparation. And he would have known she'd gone down to the big market in Marietta even if Logan Stark hadn't called to fill him in. She had skewers of marinated chicken waiting for the grill and was currently assembling all-vegetable skewers as well. To the side, he could see a potato salad waiting and understood that she'd found a way to use the food they'd had left, knowing full well that more was coming.

Because one thing he'd discovered about Kendall was that she did not like to waste things. Food most of all. Something he found he admired more than he could adequately express, even though it wouldn't have mattered if she did waste things. He could replace them.

But this way it was another chorus in that song that more and more was the only thing he heard, whether he was awake or asleep.

She glanced over and smiled. "It's ready to grill whenever you are."

And she still made no move to tell him anything, so he took the food she'd prepared outside and started the grill. When she came out and handed him the beer he liked and she'd clearly replenished down at the FlintWorks microbrewery in Marietta, he accepted it. He told her about the particular antics of the calves today. The fences that he'd repaired, because there were always fences to repair. The foolishness of his brothers, which was a favorite topic of his, though the real truth was that he didn't like to think how he'd go about handling the ranch without them. Maybe because he knew he'd never have to.

It was easier to pretend they annoyed him.

Just like it was easier not to think about the fact Zeke said he was dying.

What he found easy enough to consider instead was what his wife wasn't telling him.

When dinner was ready, they sat down at the table outside again. And Harlan was beginning to wonder if she wasn't planning to tell him anything at all.

He really hadn't expected that. It felt like a blow, and he didn't like it.

"How was the drive down to Marietta?" he asked, on the theory that maybe she needed him to start her off.

She smiled. "Fine."

"It was nice of you to do that much grocery shopping. I made sure to remind my brothers that you married me, not them, and they shouldn't take you for granted. Or give you errands to do."

"I don't mind. It's nice to feel like I'm a part of things, enough to be taken for granted a little."

He waited for her to talk about the scene Logan had witnessed, but she started talking about the conversation she'd had with his father earlier today when she'd gone by the main house to pick up their grocery list. About logos, and the name she and Zeke had come up with for their booth at the Farm and Craft market, and an aside about *bespoke cowboys* that he couldn't have followed if he tried.

Harlan felt that same, yet still unfamiliar lick of temper moving him. Because he couldn't believe that she was really, truly going to pretend it hadn't happened.

Whatever it was.

And the more she kept it to herself, the more he wanted to know why.

"So," he said when they ended up back inside after clearing the table, "do you plan to tell me about those women?"

"What women?"

But he saw the way her shoulders tensed. "You know which women."

He watched her pull in a breath. And then take her time turning to face him, likely to get her face to look that impassive. That calm. "They don't concern you. They don't concern anyone. They have nothing to do with anything that matters, and I'd like to keep it that way."

"I'm guessing they're family," Harlan said, fighting to stay calm himself.

And he watched something… detonate in her at that. He could see it in her eyes. And the way she flushed and went rigid, then folded her arms in front of her. "Why would you say that?"

"Because the guy who called to tell me about this altercation that my wife was in on the streets of Marietta, an altercation you don't seem inclined to share yourself, said they looked a lot like you."

"That's just…"

He watched her flail and felt two competing urges. One to let her, so he could see why she was doing this. And the other to protect her, even if it was from him and his questions. She sounded shakier than before when she let out what wasn't quite a laugh.

"What's funny is that they would both hate that," she said, that funny almost-laugh still in her voice. "They don't think I'm up to their standard, especially not now. I've let myself go, you see. And apparently, I was already too far gone."

"They sound like they don't know what they're talking about."

"Which is why I didn't see any reason to bring them up." She shook her head. "Yes, they're family. No, I don't want to talk about it and next time, you can tell your friend to mind his business."

"What about my business?"

She was still staring at him with that look in her eyes, hectic and something a little too close to self-loathing for his taste. "What about it? What does it have to do with you?"

"Kendall." That came out a little louder than he expected it to. And he didn't like that he raised his voice, but then again, he didn't like any part of this. "You're my wife."

"This isn't part of the deal," she threw back at him, sounding something like desperate, which he liked least of all. "They have nothing to do with anything that happens here, and that's for your protection, Harlan. You don't know what they're like." She blew out another breath, harsher than before. "It's okay. They don't know I'm married. I didn't tell them."

"Why would you think that's okay? We are married. And I don't care who you tell about it."

"You don't understand."

"You're right. I don't understand, because you haven't told me. You won't tell me. And, in fact, you've gone out of your way to avoid talking about your past at all." He folded his arms because he wanted to reach for her too badly. "I could have told you that's a surefire way to make sure your past shows up."

"You could have told me?" She laughed at that, but it was a brittle sound. "What past are you talking about? Your life of duty and family and responsibility? Your good, clean, happy life up here in these beautiful mountains, where every now and again—just to mix things up—you do something spontaneous that doesn't hurt anybody? That past, Harlan?"

She threw up her hands, and he had the sense that he was finally seeing all of her. That this woman who he'd been waiting so long to see. And it wasn't that he *wanted* to see her upset, because he didn't—but that at least, now, he knew she wasn't wearing any kind of a mask.

He wanted to tell her that, but her eyes were dark and flashing at him. "My past isn't like that," she told him. "The people I come from aren't good."

"But you are." He saw her flinch at that. "You are, Kendall. Do you think I would let you come here if you weren't? To my home? Here with all these people who matter to me? You were just telling me yesterday about how much things matter to folks around here. Do you think I'm any different?"

"I think," she said in a quiet sort of voice that didn't sound like her at all, and he hated it, "that you are a man. And men are willing to put up with a lot if it means—"

"I don't think you want to finish that sentence."

Her eyes seemed slick with misery then. Harlan could feel the shift in the air between them, how everything got stark. How even breathing seemed to hurt.

"I'm just pointing out a universal truth," she began, but it was as if the words were sour in her mouth. They sounded sour between them.

"Do you really think that I'm that hard up for a woman?" he asked her gruffly. "Of all the replies I got to that ad, yours was the only one that interested me. And I figured that we would have a meeting and I'd likely get a lot less interested, but I was willing to take that chance. And sure, I was surprised to find that you're as pretty as you are. But that's not why I married you."

"I think it's exactly why you married me," she shot back at him. "And you're proving my point."

"I want you to hear me when I say this," he said in a very low and very urgent voice, moving closer to her so he could stand right there, near enough to reach out a hand and put it on the place where her arms were still crossed. "I want you to understand why I'm saying it. There is no shortage of pretty women in the world, Kendall. And I've never had a problem talking to the ones I've been lucky enough to meet. But none of them are you."

She swayed a little at that, but she shook her head. And that defiant chin of hers went up again. "Harlan. I was there."

"There is no possible way I would have gone through with something as crazy as finding myself a mail-order bride and bringing her home," he told her flatly, his gaze hard on hers, "if it wasn't you. You have to know that."

She shook her head. Once, then again.

"This isn't helping," she said, though her voice sounded choked. Rough. "I don't know what you think is going on, but for me, none of this is worth talking about. And you saying things like this just makes it worse."

"Why?"

And Harlan could hear the dark current in his voice. The driving need to keep her safe. To make her feel better. To pull her close and show her that everything he'd told her was the truth. All those things at once, and while he was at it, an even greater need to hunt down those women and explain to them that *this* was not something he would allow.

Not his wife. Not on his watch.

"I'm not who you think I am," she told him, her voice

barely a scratch and her eyes too bright. "I don't mean that I have some fake identity or separate passport hidden away somewhere. I'm not that fancy. But this costume I've been wearing here, of this woman who could belong in a place like this? She doesn't exist."

"She's right here in front of me."

"I wish I could be her, I really do. But who am I kidding?" Her voice began to rise then, too. "Deep down, people don't ever really change. They don't. They just wish they could."

"I think they can," Harlan argued. "It takes a lot of work and a lot of determination, and to be honest, most folks don't have it in them."

She looked like that had been a sucker punch, but she was staying on her feet. Somehow. "There you go."

"So what I have to wonder, Kendall, is if it's being here that let you be the real you for the first time. If you finally dropped that costume you wore out there. No change necessary. Just... no mask."

And then he watched, in a mixture of astonishment and horror, as her face crumpled. As her shoulders shook, like a sob was ripping through her body.

"This has always been temporary," she told him, though her voice was even more ragged than before. And he could see the tears begin to streak down her cheeks. "Damn you, Harlan, this was only ever supposed to be *temporary.*"

"I didn't take *temporary* vows," he growled. "And neither

did you."

She lifted her hands to wipe at her eyes and he could see that she was shaking, buffeted by that same wind he couldn't feel.

But he could see it rip through her.

"You can trust me," he told her, another vow that wasn't the slightest bit temporary. "I promise you, whatever this is, you can trust me, Kendall."

The sound she made then was like a sob, though he could hear frustration in it too.

"Trusting you is not the problem," she told him, though she had to fight to get the words out. "Of course I can trust you. Everyone can trust you. You're *trustworthy*, Harlan. That's never going to be the problem." She pulled in a breath then. It sounded like knives. And she wasn't even pretending not to cry. Not anymore. "The problem is that you can't trust me. I'm bad, straight through."

"Bullshit," he said, succinctly.

And then he proved it to her.

He stopped playing games. He stopped waiting.

Harlan kissed her, and this time, he didn't intend to stop.

Not until she could see herself the way he did.

Chapter Nine

THIS KISS WAS different.

This kiss was scalding, pouring into her and through her, until Kendall wasn't sure she could survive it.

But then, she was equally unsure if she wanted to.

She knew that the smart thing to do was not to cling to him like this. She knew that the wise move was to pull away, not melt against him.

Then again, this was Harlan.

And Kendall couldn't bear the thought that this was ending, this thing between them.

Though she knew, beyond any shadow of a doubt and despite any vows this man might like to make, that it was.

She knew exactly what it meant that her mother and sister had found her here. Kendall had understood two things the moment she'd seen them. Before they'd opened up their mouths and confirmed for her, as always, that they were just as awful as she remembered them.

First, that she would do whatever she had to do to make absolutely certain they never made it up the hill to Cowboy Point. Much less onto the ranch.

Second, that she would protect Harlan from them if it

was the last thing she did in this life.

And if saving him meant that she had to give him up and go back to them the way she always did, so they would be none the wiser and never know he existed, she would do that, too.

God, she didn't know how she would do that—

But she would. She could be that strong.

Kendall knew she could, and that she would, but she also knew that she wasn't strong enough to deny him this.

Not this thing she'd wanted too much and for too long herself. Not this thing that had been brewing between them since the moment she'd stepped into that saloon in Marietta.

Maybe even sooner than that, because she still didn't know what had compelled her to answer his ad in the first place.

All of this flashed through her in an instant.

And what Kendall thought, above all, was *I don't care about consequences.*

Because he was kissing her again. At last.

He was kissing her *like this* and she wished with every particle of her being that she could kiss him *like this* forever.

And so, for a moment, Kendall did exactly what she wanted. She stopped worrying. She stopped piecing together her own unpleasant future. She stopped worrying about the same thing she always and ever worried about.

She was here, now.

So she melted into him.

Harlan's arms came around her immediately. He pulled her up higher against his chest, then lifted her off the ground so he could carry her over and set her on the counter behind them.

Then he stepped between her legs and everything got hotter.

Deeper.

Wilder.

She slid her hands to his jaw, and then she kissed him over and over. It was a glorious thing to hold his face between her hands. To feel the rough texture of his jaw. To run her fingers into that thick, dirty-blond hair that felt so soft against her palms.

Though *soft* wasn't quite the right word, because the more she luxuriated in his different textures while his mouth did such marvelous, magical things to hers, the more the fire in her took her over.

The flames seemed to dance and weave over every inch of her body, singeing her from her bones on out.

His hands moved from her back, skimming his way along the sides of her body as if he was learning her in braille. She bloomed beneath his touch, as if she was becoming a brand-new person simply because he was touching her. That he was somehow *making* her into the wife she ought to be, the one who would deserve to kiss him like this in this kitchen they shared.

She had never wanted anything more than to be that

woman. That wife.

Then his hands were on her thighs and that was *impossible*. Impossibly *good*. It was a delicious, drugging heat that was almost shocking in its intensity. It was like throwing gasoline on an open flame and until this moment Kendall hadn't known such a sharp, bright pleasure was *possible*.

She didn't know how on earth she was going to survive this.

But the more it went on, the more she figured she actually didn't want to survive it at all. She wanted to lose herself in this. In him.

She wanted to stay right here. Forever.

And if that wasn't on offer? Well, she had no one but herself to blame for that. She'd known that going in.

There was no use crying over spilt milk. Especially not when they could be kissing instead.

Still, when he pulled back—his breath coming as heavy and as ragged as hers—she felt more like crying than she ever had in her life.

Maybe she already was.

"You don't taste like a problem," Harlan told her, and his voice was a revelation. That same, deep rumble. Maybe a little darker now, and a little deeper. But it was like she could *feel* his voice in all the places where he'd made her bloom. "You taste like you belong right here, no matter what."

And that broke her heart in pieces.

She felt her eyes well up with tears all over again, but she couldn't even muster up her usual horror at that. Maybe she really did trust him.

To be, at the very least, not her mother or sister. He wouldn't see her tears as a weakness. He wouldn't use her feelings against her as a weapon.

And even as she thought that, he proved it. Harlan ran his thumb under one eye and then the other. He caught the moisture beneath both.

And then he looked at her as if she was too precious to bear.

Her poor heart was never going to recover.

"I married you under false pretenses," she told him. She waited for him to react to that, but all he did was stand where he was, pressed up against her here at the counter in their kitchen—his kitchen, she corrected herself—his gaze as steady as before. "I expected you to be sad and weird."

"And very old."

"And that." She swallowed hard. "I figured I could dance around these various intimacies and get a little vacation from my real life either way."

That intent dark gaze never changed, and yet somehow that felt encouraging. She told herself that the absence of an attack didn't make something *supportive*. Not really.

Still, it made her feel safe.

Or he did, so maybe that was the same thing, in the end.

And no wonder she was having trouble recognizing it. When had she ever felt anything even approximating *safe* before?

But she made herself keep going. "I figured… no harm, no foul. The kind of man who advertises for a wife in a newspaper can't be too surprised if that wife disappears one day. That's all I was going to do. Retreat for a while, get back on my feet, lick my wounds a little. And then go. Clean and easy."

"I sure hope this feeling is as muddy to you as it is to me," he said then, in that low voice that rumbled all the way through her and made her shivery and hot.

And she suspected he knew it did. It was there in that crook in the corner of his mouth. It was in the way he smoothed his hand over her hair while the other one stayed where it was, hot and heavy on her thigh. High on her thigh.

Not moving, just *there*.

As if he was claiming her like that.

And the funny thing was, her entire body responded to this—to *him*, to whatever he was doing, to the *fact* of him—with delight.

Bright, hot, endless delight.

"Muddier by the second," she whispered. "But you don't deserve that."

"I don't wait around much, concerned about getting what I *deserve*," Harlan drawled. "I make things happen and see where that gets me instead."

And Kendall wanted to melt into him again. It would be so easy. She felt the pull of him, an irresistible force—

She propped her hands against his chest so she could make her own barrier, if necessary. One she might actually obey.

"Harlan." His name was starting to feel like its own sort of fire in her mouth, and the way he smiled at her didn't help. "It never occurred to me that you, a man I met through an ad like that, would be... Well, *you*. I never thought I'd like your home. Your family. This whole community. I'm not that type of person. I don't put down roots. The first hint that I might attach to something and I leave."

"Kendall," he said softly. "We're already married. That's about as attached as you can get."

"I knew before I started that I was going to go," she told him, and it felt like the terrible confession it was. "This is what I'm trying to tell you. It wasn't that I thought I *might* feel like leaving someday, so I was giving myself an out. It was a plan. I thought it would be a couple of weeks. A month at the most. And here we are coming to the end of July." She shook her head, much too aware of how hard his chest was beneath her hands, how hot. And how difficult it was to keep her hands in one place instead of letting them wander. "Even if my past hadn't showed up I'd still be getting out of here. However you look at it, time's up."

She expected him to step away, but he didn't. He was Harlan, so he stepped closer. And as he gathered her up in his arms all over again and kissed her like she hadn't just said she was leaving him, his taste flooded through her.

But so did the fact of what she'd just told him. The details she'd shared.

Because in a way—in her way—she'd declared her love, hadn't she?

A Darlington never told anyone their plans. They never let anyone in on their schemes. Accordingly, they had no friends, no intimates, nothing. There was family and then there was everyone else. And family might stab you in the back, but everyone else was a mark.

And yet, somehow, Kendall had carved out a space for Harlan inside of her, separate from either of those.

Not just for Harlan, she realized as she leaned in closer and wrapped her arms around his neck, so she could give as good as she got in this glorious kiss that went on and on and on and used most of both of their bodies.

There was a perfect little mountain valley that she'd fit in to that space between the two extremes that governed her life. She hadn't even realized she was doing it.

She loved it here.

It was that simple.

She loved it here, with these people and with him, and she'd been changing her whole life and the way she lived since he'd brought her up to the backside of Copper Mountain almost three months ago now.

And it was only possible, she understood as that fire crackled through her and the flames between them reached so high, because somewhere along the way she'd fallen in love with him.

Everything about Cowboy Point seemed bright and golden to her because every day was bookended with him. The beginning and the end of everything was Harlan.

Their quiet, happy mornings. The days they spent together, the days spent apart, and the evenings she couldn't wait for. Talking with him. Laughing with him. Staring up at that summer sky and telling each other stories.

Whether they were sitting out behind his house or involving themselves in the summer joy that the whole community shared, it didn't matter.

It was all about him.

Kendall had understood that he would wreck her from the first moment she'd laid eyes on him, and she'd gone ahead and sat down with him anyway.

So there was no doubt. This was her fault.

She pulled away this time, though she didn't get far. Maybe she couldn't bear to pull herself *too* far away from him. She rested her forehead on his and fought for air while their lips were only a breath apart.

"Harlan," she began.

"Baby," he replied, she could hear something different in his voice, something that made her think she might not recognize herself when she was done with this. With him. That she might leave, but she wouldn't be taking all of her when she went. And the words he said next made that clear. "Truth is, I don't care. It doesn't matter. Only you matter.

Here. With me. Everything else, we can fix."

"We can't." She shook her head. "I'm telling you, I have to go."

He called her baby again, in that same voice. And it tore her apart and then filled her up again, with a brighter light than any she'd ever known.

"Baby. Kendall." His hands were in her hair. His big body was between her legs. "Stay."

And she knew better, she really did, but in that moment she couldn't do a single thing but melt into him all over again.

This time he picked her up in his arms and carried her through the house, taking her back into his bedroom where she'd never been.

A glance around told her it was the same as the rest of the house. Comfortable. Masculine. Huge windows to let the wilderness in and another massive fireplace to keep the long winters at bay. Books on built-in shelves, richly patterned rugs on the wood floors, and a terrace all to himself.

She immediately felt at home.

And that didn't change when he lay her down on his big, wide bed and crawled his way up the length of her body so they could kiss a while like that, too. With her wrapped all around him and his weight pressing her down, setting off a new series of detonations that she thought might very well kill her, they were so intense. So perfect.

Everything got blurry and wild and when he pulled

away, his hand was splayed out over her belly, beneath her shirt.

She wanted it lower.

"I need you naked," he told her, his voice a gravelly thing.

"You first," she dared him.

They both sat up at the same time. And they were laughing as they pulled off their clothes in a hurry, tossing them all into a tangle beside the bed.

Then there was just... the *expanse* of him.

God help her, but Harlan was a sight to see.

That he'd spent his life working the land, and much of it with his own hands, was immediately obvious. He was all ridged muscles and obvious strength, and she felt a wonderful sort of dizzy just looking at the hair on his chest and the way it seemed to form an irresistible arrow down to where the proudest part of him stood tall and ready.

She moved forward, reaching out to wrap her hand around him, and felt the thrill of a particularly feminine triumph in the way he pulled in a sharp breath at the contact.

He stood there by the side of the bed and let her learn the shape of him, thick and hot and hard.

But when she moved as if to take him into her mouth, he laughed.

"The first thing we're going to do," he told her, moving closer and tipping her back with his momentum, so she tumbled over and he followed her down, "is make sure you come. Again and again. I've been wanting a taste of you since the day we met."

"I have too," she retorted.

He grinned at her, this man who said he didn't compete because he always won. "Tough."

And the way he took control then left her in no doubt that he'd been treating her gently and oh, so carefully, before. The contrast was like being dipped in a thick, molten fire, and she loved it. She exulted in it.

Harlan rolled her where he wanted her, then shifted down the length of her body. He took hold of her legs and draped them up and over his wide, hard shoulders. He spread her thighs open even wider before him and then settled in, licking his way into her with absolutely no preamble.

She shattered, instantly, as his hot, impossible mouth tore her apart with every graze of his tongue against the place where she was softest. Hottest.

Kendall arched up against him. She heard the sound of her own voice rising in a wail, a sob—

But all Harlan did was keep holding her where he wanted her, letting her buck up against his face.

He kept right on going.

And she had no choice, so she did too.

Gloriously.

Not content to make her shatter one way, he used his

fingers, too, making low noises of approval and encouragement as he took her up that cliff, and threw her over.

Again and again and again.

Kendall was wrung out, limp and sobbing and clinging to him as if he was the only solid ground in the whole world, when he finally crawled his way up the length of her body. And then settled between her legs, so she could feel his hardness against all that molten heat he'd made.

She took hold of his head and pulled it to her, kissing him as if her life depended on it. Tasting herself, and heat, and him.

God, and *him*.

And she was moving against him, sliding against that rock-hard part of him, driving herself wild all over again.

She had the thought that she really ought to insist that they use something, but the thought of any barrier between them made her want to die.

So she reached down between them, took him in her fist once more, and then—at last—guided him to her core.

They both felt the way he notched the thick head of himself inside her. She held her breath. He tensed, everywhere.

And then, that intense gaze of his on hers, he pressed in.

Deeper, then deeper still, so she lifted up her hips to take more of him.

Until, finally, he filled her completely.

And they both went still. The pounding of their hearts

was so loud, almost overwhelming, and Kendall could *feel* her pulse everywhere they touched.

Or maybe it was his pulse.

But there was something too good about the way they were joined, like a fist in a glove.

Perfect, something in her whispered.

Only then, only when she started pressing against him, urging him on, did he begin to move.

And nothing in her whole life, not even the things he'd already done with his mouth, could possibly have prepared her for this.

For Harlan, her husband, so deep inside her body that she knew she was never going to be the same again.

For this sheer, sweet perfection of his body and hers and the way they fit together.

Every thrust was a revelation.

She could feel him everywhere, inside and out, again and again.

Sensation took her over, spinning them both far, far away like they were hurled out into that big sky somewhere above them.

But he was Harlan, so he took his time.

He was careful, methodical, and he drove her wild.

He pounded into her, brought her close to the edge— and then shifted back to a lazy, maddening, beautiful pace that made her cry out. And sometimes use her teeth. And call him names that made him laugh.

Again and again he did this, until she could no longer tell the difference between coming and not coming.

She was sobbing, she was saying his name. And she thought it was possible she said far more telling things than that, the words she'd promised herself she would never say out loud—

But then it stopped mattering.

Because he found the highest peak of all and grinned, then sent her catapulting off the side of it, out into everything.

Flying, not falling.

He wrapped her up, put his mouth to her ear, and said the thing he had to know changed everything, even then.

"I love you," Harlan whispered. "I love you, Kendall. Stay with me."

Over and over again.

As they both flew off into the wonder of it all together, like they had wings to spare and nothing but eternity ahead.

Chapter Ten

I N THE MORNING, Harlan woke at his usual time and left her in his bed.

Where she belonged and would stay, if he had anything to say on the subject.

And he hoped he did, because he already found it deeply satisfying to go out and do a round of chores before dawn, then come back to find her in his kitchen. He found he spent the whole day looking forward to coming back to her at night.

But there was nothing to compare to the sight of his wife, naked and her hair a mess, curled up in his own bed.

She was still asleep when he got back and that pleased him, too. He took the opportunity to make her some of the coffee she liked better than his, which was more like jet fuel. And while he was at it, he scrambled up some eggs and fried some bacon, then arranged it on a plate with some toast. Then he carried it all into the bedroom.

Kendall sat up with a jolt when he set the plate down on his bedside table. Then she looked around in alarm, as if she hadn't meant to fall asleep last night. Or early this morning, to be more precise, because they'd reached for each other again and again.

He couldn't say he liked the fact that she looked like she still didn't mean to stay.

"Harlan," she began, in that tone that suggested she was going to tell him things he wasn't going to like.

He nodded toward the food and the coffee, crossed the room to settle into the big armchair near the window with his own mug.

"You better eat before you set about breaking my heart," he told her in a drawl.

And he found he liked the flush that moved over her at that, starting in her cheeks and then washing down to her breasts, too. Painting her in pretty colors like his own, personal sunrise.

It was harder than he'd care to admit to stay in his chair when he knew how she tasted. And the weight of her breast against his palm. And the sounds she made when he was deep inside her.

Like she was remembering the same things, Kendall swallowed hard. She pulled the sheets up around her body like that might make either one of them forget, but then she did what he told her. She took a long pull from the mug of coffee. And then, with only a glance his way, she started eating.

He wasn't surprised that she was hungry. It had been a long night. Harlan wasn't sure he had slept at all himself, though he was equally sure he'd never felt better.

When she was finished eating, Kendall sat back against the headboard. She let out a long sigh that a lesser man might have taken as a bad sign, but Harlan wasn't interested in *signs*. Today he was all about intentions. Reality.

And making the wife he hadn't expected to fall in love with see a little reason.

Kendall pulled the sheets and the blanket up to her chin, and, for a moment, looked like the little girl she must have been. Once upon a time.

He decided, then and there, that he would be perfectly happy to have a fleet of little girls that looked just like her. Dark hair. Big eyes.

That smile he'd seen too many times to count last night.

But he knew better than to say something like that. Kendall still looked spooked, like she might run at any moment. He didn't want that.

He wanted her.

All of her.

"I think it's time that you tell me everything," he said then.

She seemed to freeze at that. But she nodded. "I will." She pulled her bottom lip between her teeth, then let it go. "And if after I explain, you want to take back the things you said last night... I'll understand."

Harlan laughed, loud enough that she looked startled. "That I love you? Do you think that's the kind of thing that comes and goes so easily?" He shook his head. "There's not a single thing you could tell me that would make me stop loving you, Kendall. I promise you that."

But that only made her look more miserable. "How about this? I'm a bad person."

"I don't agree." Harlan shrugged when she frowned at him. "You can say that if you want. I can't stop you. But if you want me to agree with you? Baby, you're going to have to prove it."

She scowled at that, but she didn't respond. Not directly. Instead, she spent a moment or two knotting her hair on the back of her head.

And he had to order himself not to get distracted by all that glossy, pretty hair of hers, that he could still almost feel trailing across his skin, driving him wild.

He believed there would be more of that.

Hell, he would make sure there was.

Kendall didn't seem to realize that Harlan Carey wasn't going to let her go without a fight.

"I never knew my father," she said after a moment. "Or I guess I might have, but no one man was ever positively identified as the actual, lucky winner of that prize. Some of the earliest things I remember involve my mother pretending that different men might be responsible for me. And then my sister a few years later. That's what we did in Nashville. And all over Tennessee. And then throughout the whole South. Mama would go around making this man or that worry about paternity. That was her favorite scam and she played around with it for most of our childhood."

She kept looking at him for a reaction, so he kept his face impassive. But he doubted that he was responding the way she clearly expected. He wasn't sure he had a single negative thought about a child who'd been used like that by her own mother. How was it the child's fault?

Though Harlan found he did have a lot of thoughts, however, about a mother who would play games like that with her own children. Using them as pawns.

Or even weapons.

"As we got older, my sister Breanna really became my mother's protégé. She's the pretty one." Kendall's mouth curved, but if that was a smile, it was the bleakest one he'd ever seen. "And I don't say that to get down on myself. I like my own looks just fine. But there's a certain kind of pretty that can be utilized, you see. A certain kind of pretty that could make us money and that was Breanna, not me."

"I want to be clear on what you mean by that," he said, slowly.

Carefully.

She smiled. Another one that got nowhere near her eyes.

"I don't actually know what boundaries my sister has," she said after a moment. "I know that she and my mother like to target men. Sometimes together, sometimes alone. If you're asking me if they sell themselves, it's not that straight-forward. The simple answer is no. What they do is create a scenario, then extract a price." She held his gaze for a long moment. A breath, maybe. "They prefer married men for that reason."

He could see the way she tensed at that and it took him a moment to understand why.

"Kendall." Harlan had to go easy, and he had to caution himself that this wasn't a reflection on him. This was what she feared, not what he'd shown her. He couldn't lose his cool now. "Is part of the reason you think you have to leave is because you think they can play their games with me?"

He saw the jolt that went through her, that she tried to hide. Just like he could see the sheer misery in her gaze. "This is the family business. They're good at it."

"It sounds to me like what they're good at is finding weak men and exploiting that weakness." He kept his gaze on her, steady and true. "But that's not going to work on me."

She did not look as comforted by that as he would have liked. "Aren't you going to ask me how I contributed to Darlington family enterprise?"

"I'm not going to ask you." He sat forward, still keeping his gaze trained on hers like his life depended on it. Because it did. "You can tell me if you want. But I know who you are, Kendall."

She made a soft sound. "You really don't."

"I've watched the way you took on life here. How you made friends when you didn't have to, and especially not when you thought you were leaving soon. You made my father feel alive again when we don't know how much time he has left. You've involved yourself in the community. The ranch. The family. Like these things matter to you."

"That could be an act for all you know."

"I don't think so. You take care of people. Of me. Of this house. Of the business. I have to assume that's the same kind of thing you did for your mother and your sister, even if, in my opinion, they don't deserve it. Or you, if it got you running scared like this."

She let out a broken sort of sound and put her hands over her face. "I'm the one who fixes things," she said through her fingers. "I'm the one who keeps situations from getting too... intense. They're good at what they do, I suppose, but then I go in and clean it up."

"It's like what I hear you told my dad," Harlan said. "You're good at sales."

Kendall lifted her head and there were tears streaming down her face. "I don't understand this. Why are you being so nice to me? I'm sitting here telling you I come from a family of grifters and con-women, and you are..."

"In love with you, Kendall." Harlan said it very calmly. Very distinctly, so there could be no doubt. "I said it in bed last night and I meant it. But I imagine you're already dismissing that, because I'd bet you've heard a lot of men say those things to your mother or your sister in similar situations. And you knew perfectly well that it couldn't be love. That it wasn't in all those scenarios." He nodded when another sobbing sort of sound escaped her. "But baby, this is you and me. This is the real deal."

"My family—" she began.

"I'm your family," Harlan told her, with finality.

And the way she looked at him then, with terror and wonder all over her lovely face, he had no choice but to go over to her.

He crawled on to the bed with her, scooped her up, and twisted them both around until he could hold her on his lap. He smoothed her hair back from her hot face, and then he kissed her.

Once. Again.

"Here's what I think should happen." He tucked her against his chest, resting his chin on the top of her head. And he smiled when he felt her hand move, as if to hold his heart in her palm. "Because I can't have my wife panic like this. I can't have these people showing up and making you doubt who you are. I think you should invite them to the ranch. We can all sit down and have a talk about reality. And what that looks like."

Kendall pulled back then and looked at him with horror all over her face.

"Oh no. You can't do that. I can't let them anywhere near you."

Harlan kissed her. "Invite them over, baby," he told her, a soft order but an order all the same. "They're not dealing with you anymore. Or not *just* you."

But this was Kendall, who doubted who she was. Or didn't understand. Not yet.

Harlan vowed that she would.

Today.

Because this was going to be the last time she stared at him blankly when he reminded her who, exactly, she was now.

"You're a Carey, Kendall." When she blinked at that, then flushed with pleasure—the way he liked best—he smiled wider. "And one thing you should know about us Careys is that we always, *always*, take care of our own."

Chapter Eleven

I N THE END, Kendall convinced Harlan that it was unwise to let Mayrose and Breanna actually *see* the ranch.

"I understand what you're going for, but the last thing you need is them actually grasping what a ranch is, what you do here, and... all of this." They were in the living room then and she'd waved her hands around in all directions, trying to take in the mountains, the pastures. All that *land*. "We'll never be rid of them."

Part of her expected him to wave that away like the rest of her objections, but he didn't. And she gave herself a stern talking-to about categorizing him like that. He hadn't waved away anything she'd said, ever. Now, like then, he considered it.

This time, he nodded.

"And to be honest," she said when he did, "I'm not sure you should let them come up to Cowboy Point, either. Marietta is close enough."

"Marietta isn't ours," Harlan said.

And that was how they decided to ask her mother and sister to meet them at Mountain Mama that afternoon.

"This is actually humiliating," Kendall told Flannery

when she went in to ask if they wouldn't mind letting her take over some space even though it was summer. The middle of their busiest season. "My family is terrible. We're meeting in public so they can't do as much damage as they might do otherwise. I can't imagine why you'd want that cluttering up your happy restaurant, to be honest."

She tensed, expecting that this woman she'd privately—hopefully—wondered if she might make into a friend would get chilly with her and put some distance between them, but Flannery didn't do that. She stepped closer instead and pressed her shoulder to Kendall's.

"Someday, we'll sit down and tell each other stories about how we ended up on the far side of a Rocky Mountain peak far, far away from our families of origin. Because believe you me, mine is no picnic either."

It was a gift. Kendall tucked it away in her heart that was already overflowing with the things that Harlan had said to her. With that first night and that morning after and the magic of every moment since.

With the notion that he was her family now.

And with a sense of sheer, giddy wonder about what that might mean.

She felt so plush with these gifts that it was close enough to easy to call her sister when she got back to the house and extend the invitation that she would rather not have had to extend at all.

Though at least they wouldn't be coming *here*, she

thought, looking up at the house she shared with Harlan. At least she could keep this sacred.

"You're inviting us to *pizza?*" Breanna asked, laughing. It was not a nice laugh. "Is that a euphemism?"

"It's a meal," Kendall said dryly.

"This is so typical," Mayrose said then, obviously snatching the phone away from Breanna. "Do you really think we didn't have anything better to do than chase you all over the state of Montana? It's summer, Kendall. And thanks to your selfishness, we're shuffling around cold mountain towns instead of bustling, sparkling, gleaming resort towns near the ocean. I hope you're proud."

"You're welcome to take yourself off to any beach you like, Mama," Kendall gritted back at her. "With my compliments."

Breanna took the phone again. "Now you've done it. She's in a rage."

Kendall had been pacing back and forth in front of the house while she made this call, aware that Harlan was watching her from inside. Letting her have her space while he made a few calls of his own. Because really, as far she could tell, he might be the perfect man.

And she didn't need him hearing what sounded like Mayrose's patented scream-into-the-pillow performance that had always terrified her as a child.

"How did you find me anyway?" she asked her sister.

"I've been tracking your phone for years," Breanna said

with a certain offhandedness that made everything inside Kendall just... go cold. "You're always much too squirrely."

"*Squirrely,*" Kendall repeated, though her lips felt numb.

"I assume that wherever you are now is out of range, but we tracked you to Livingston easily enough. Then here to this little Podunk town. Bozeman, then back."

Breanna sounded careless and breezy, but Kendall knew her sister. And so she knew that Breanna wanted to make sure Kendall knew that they'd been on her from the start. That she'd never actually escaped them. That any sense of freedom she'd had was a lie.

"We spent a lot of time in Bozeman," her sister was saying, and this made sense to Kendall. There were very wealthy people in Bozeman and therefore better hunting for the Darlingtons. "I'm betting this Cowboy Point of yours is up some mountain, isn't it? It's impossible to track you until you come back down."

"Good to know."

"Thing is, we want to move on," Breanna said, her voice less breezy, now. "Montana is a drag."

Kendall looked around, unable to imagine what her sister was talking about. She thought that she would want to live right here, on this hill with its stunning views, crisp mountain air, and the smell of the pines in everything, whether she was with Harlan or not. And she knew that if she left this place, she would grieve it for the rest of her life.

She would dream about it every night, always.

And that was just the actual *place*. The trees, the craggy skyline, the dirt.

That wasn't even getting into all the other things she'd miss.

"You can come meet me today, in exactly one hour, or you can take the easier option and go away right now without bothering to meet up," Kendall told her sister, in a calm voice that she was inordinately proud of. "Those are your choices and in neither of them will I be going with you. Just so we're clear."

"We'll see about that," her sister said in that singsong voice of hers that always heralded her being absolutely horrible.

So Kendall got ahead of that and hung up. She stared down at the phone in her hand and frowned, then looked up how to remove any sort of tracking software. She followed the directions, squatting down on the steps that led up to the front door.

And while she turned off the various location services and checked for tracking apps, she tried to get herself to calm down.

"All set?" Harlan asked from behind her.

She turned, and wondered if she would always lose her breath a little at the sight of him. Jeans and a Stetson and all that *Harlan* in between. If they had more than an hour, she would have suggested they revisit some of last night's high points.

Instead, she nodded. "They're coming."

His dark eyes gleamed. "Good."

And then she got another gift when they headed down into Cowboy Point, because Harlan's entire family came with them. They were all waiting at the main house, and followed Harlan's truck all the way to Mountain Mama's.

All of his brothers. Zeke and Belinda. Once they made it to the pizza place, they all rolled in and assembled themselves like a wall of Careys in the dining room, where Flannery had said they could have this meeting.

Kendall stared at them, pretty sure that her jaw had actually dropped open.

"Didn't Harlan tell you?" Wilder asked, with that lazy grin of his that she noticed, the way she always did but even more so today, in no way made him seem less dangerous. "You're family, Kendall."

"And in this family," Zeke said with a certain placidity that was completely undercut by the look in his eyes, "it's all for one and one for all."

Kendall had never felt anything like this in her life. This high tide of hope and *what if*. She wanted to give each and every one of her in-laws a hug. She wanted to promise them that if the time came, she would wade into battle for them in a heartbeat.

But all she could seem to manage was a watery smile.

"You got this," Knox told her.

"And we got you," Boone agreed.

Kendall almost forgot why they were gathered here, but then the door to Mountain Mama's opened and in came Mayrose and Breanna, as slinky and terrible as ever.

They didn't look any different. Kendall wasn't sure why she'd thought they should. Mayrose was still dedicated to her engine-red hair that she wore in a cloud all around her, always a counterpoint to her pale ivory skin. Breanna maintained her golden brush of a tan and a perfect blowout no matter what, and these days spent a lot of time plumping up her lips.

Full of sharks, Kendall thought. *That's what they are no matter what they look like.*

"My goodness," purred her mother as she floated in, wearing a pair of jeans that showed off every square inch of her body, a crop top that showed off more, and a pair of heels that could not have been more out of place on the top of this mountain if she'd tried. "You brought a whole crowd of big, strong men to protect you against us? Little old *us*?"

Kendall could feel herself bristle as she watched the pair of them size up each member of the Carey family. She wanted to stand between Mayrose and the line of them. She wanted to slap that assessing look off her sister's face.

And that was new. Normally, she just... shut down in the presence of her mother and sister. Because there was no point fighting with them. There never had been.

Kendall never won. It was impossible to win a fight with people who only cared about causing pain, who never let anything go, and who, in the end, only ever thought about themselves.

But this wasn't just about her. *She* could put up with the Darlingtons. She'd been one herself for the whole of her life. She'd learned how to protect herself as much as possible when they were around.

You're not a Darlington anymore, she reminded herself.

And that made all the difference.

Because today was about these people who she'd come to like so much. To care for. And in Harlan's case, to love.

There was no way that she was going to let them treat these people—*her* people—the way they treated everyone else.

"Who are all these big, strong strangers, Kendall?" Mayrose asked, in that cutesy, little girl voice of hers.

Kendall took a quick glance around and was pleased to see that every last one of her in-laws looked as put off by Mayrose's act as she was.

Maybe Harlan was right. Maybe it wasn't *men* her mother and sister preyed on.

Just the weak ones.

"Kendall is my wife," Harlan told them, with that drawl of his somehow making the announcement seem more official.

And he waited there with that intent, stern look on his face when Breanna and Mayrose looked at each other, then fell about laughing.

When Kendall made a move as if she was going to either go over to them, or yell at them to stop, he settled his hand on the nape of her neck and kept her where she was.

Tucked up next to him like she'd been made to fit right there. "Is something funny?" he asked.

With a deadly sort of calm that made all of his brothers wince.

"Your wife?" Breanna repeated. She trilled out another laugh. "Oh please. What scam is this?"

"It's not a scam," Kendall replied, because she couldn't help herself. "You wouldn't understand that, I know."

But she realized that she wasn't shut down.

She didn't feel dead inside at all.

In fact, it was the opposite.

"You look well-nourished," Mayrose purred, which was her way of saying that Kendall had put on weight. A deadly insult in their ranks, though today, Kendall took it as a compliment. Because she *was* well-nourished, inside and out. She wasn't the same person who had run away from Idaho. From them.

"After all these years, I guess you really did figure out how to live on your own, without us." Mayrose continued, batting her extremely fake eyelashes in an overly innocent way that put Kendall's teeth on edge. "Or maybe you had some help? You never have been any good at independence, have you?"

Kendall knew this playbook inside and out. What normally happened when Mayrose put on her act was that men leaped to do her bidding. They normally fawned all over her. And no matter what she might have been doing, or what game she was already playing, she usually walked away with a few more prospects.

Men like to imagine they can take care of you no matter what standard of care you require, Mayrose had always told them growing up. *Testosterone is so cute.*

Kendall didn't fully realize that she was braced for this very thing to happen—for chivalry to take over and make the men behind her bend over backwards to get Mayrose batting those eyelashes in their direction—until nobody moved.

Not a single member of the Carey family took even a small step forward.

And on the other side of the dining room were the big barn doors that were opened wide to let the summer in, and allow free-flowing access to the patio. Kendall could see other folks from Cowboy Point there, drifting closer with arms crossed. The cold-eyed Jack Stark and a mess of his cousins. The deputy sheriff. Cat from the General Store and Helena from the coffee cart, who, in her emotional state, she thought looked surprisingly alike standing side by side.

Even Dallas and Tennessee Lisle, who normally did nothing but look at Kendall with suspicion, were there, aiming those suspicious looks at Breanna and Mayrose for a change.

In fact, Kendall realized as her heart seemed to stutter in

her chest, everyone she'd met in Cowboy Point was here. The pastor and his wife. The artists whose jewelry and ceramics and paintings she'd oohed and aahed over at the market. Some folks from the ranches and communities even farther out.

They all crowded around the opening, looking unwelcoming—and they were aiming that look at Kendall's relatives. It was like they could see right through this act that always played well in motel bars and grubby casinos in midsized cities.

But this, Kendall thought, was Cowboy Point, where folks liked where they lived and looked after it, too.

It had never crossed her mind that might apply to her, too.

Mayrose didn't notice, so focused was she on the Carey men lined up before her like a prize. Breanna was the one who looked around, frowning a little, because it was so unusual to lose the interest of a roomful of men.

"I reckon there's been a misunderstanding," Harlan said in his low voice that somehow managed to silence the whole room and outside, too. "We didn't invite you here so you could play your usual games. I wanted to meet my in-laws. And make it as clear as I can that Kendall won't be involved with any of the things you've got cooking from this point forward."

Mayrose went from helpless and slinky to outraged in a single blink.

"I don't believe you speak for my daughter," she replied, with a lot less of that thicker-than-molasses drawl than normal.

"He can speak for me if he wants to," Kendall jumped in then. "And believe me, he's being a lot nicer than I would be."

She watched her mother consider that. She watched Mayrose glance around, finally reading the whole room as well as the patio.

Like clockwork, on came the waterworks.

"After all I've done for you," Mayrose began in a trembling voice.

"That's not going to work, Mama," Kendall told her, softly.

And she kept waiting for the townspeople to look at her in that speculative way people did sometimes, when the Darlingtons had gone too far in a single community. She kept waiting for it to be made clear that she was at least *part* of the problem, but no one was looking at her like that.

They were hardly looking at her at all. They were all studying Mayrose and Breanna in the same flinty manner.

"Thing is," interjected the deputy sheriff from over by the door, and Kendall found she got a kick out of the way both her sister and her mother flinched when they saw the star on his chest, "we don't like it when troublemakers come up here to Cowboy Point. Not to say we don't have our own brand of trouble, but we don't like to import it. And I've heard some reports about ladies meeting your description down in the Graff in Marietta the last week or so. I bet that if I put my mind to it, I could trace a path of destruction all the way back to where you came from. Bozeman, most recently?" Atticus Wayne shook his head. "Maybe I'll go ahead and do that anyway."

"One thing that's not going to happen is you staying here," Kendall told them, just to make that abundantly clear.

The deputy sheriff nodded. "We don't do your kind of trouble in Cowboy Point, ladies."

"This is a family matter," Mayrose said, her immediately tearless eyes narrowing.

"I have a family now," Kendall replied. "A real family."

And that felt terrifying. To open her mouth like that, in front of the entire community, and claim the Careys—

"Always wanted a daughter," Zeke barked out then, and Kendall thought she might actually tip over. Or dissolve into those tears that threatened the back of her eyes. Or maybe they were already tipping over, tracking heat down her cheeks. "Seems to me I got the best of them right here."

"I have too many brothers," Wilder added, and it was fascinating to see all of his intent and wickedness untempered by any curve to his mouth. He was just as much of a force as his older brother, Kendall thought. Maybe more so, in his way, because he wasn't as patient—that was clear. "Have to say, I'm loving having a sister."

"Same," Boone belted out. With Knox right behind him.

And then, as if to remove any possible remaining doubt, Belinda stepped forward, and grabbed Kendall's hand in hers.

"Go on then," she said to Mayrose, woman to woman. "Get going. You can come back one day, if and when you're ready to be a grandmother. But not before. Do you understand me?"

Kendall almost felt as if she was floating up above everyone, looking down at the scene unfolding here. This scene that was her life, somehow, but was also as close to a high-noon shootout in a Wild West town as she was likely to encounter.

The old Kendall would have crumbled.

Today's Kendall stood tall.

Mayrose was spluttering and trying to talk back to Belinda's quiet toughness.

But it was Breanna's gaze that Kendall caught then.

"You were never any good at this anyway," her sister said, shaking her head. "We've been carting your dead weight around for years."

"Then I guess congratulations are in order," Kendall replied, without a single shred of regret. "You're footloose and fancy free, Breanna. The way you've always wanted."

"We will come back," her sister singsonged. "I can promise you that. And maybe not when you have a crowd around you to make you feel big."

And there was a part of Kendall that wanted to challenge

that. A part that wanted to step forward and say something cutting right back so her sister could feel what that was like, for a change.

Yet another part of her, the bigger part, couldn't quite get there.

Because she knew the life that Breanna was clinging to so tightly. She'd lived it all these years. It had been all she knew, too.

But she'd seen that ad and she'd imagined something else.

And she'd traded that bleak, sad life in for Harlan's hand on the nape of her neck. Belinda's fierce grip on her hand. And a wall of caring men standing behind her.

While all around, the rest of this magical little valley stood ready, as if all they needed was one signal from her to handle the rest of this themselves.

Kendall had Harlan. Breanna had nothing at all. Just Mayrose's increasingly erratic behavior and a lifestyle that revolved entirely around coercing others and trading on her looks.

A life that was fading away in front of them. Kendall thought they all knew that.

So it didn't hurt her any to be kind.

"If you ever want to come back here and try being a real sister, you're welcome to," Kendall told her. "The door is always open."

"But if you take that as an invitation to come see what

you can lift, I'd advise against it," Harlan added in that drawl of his. "This is Montana. We don't take kindly to rustlers or thieves of any description."

Breanna scoffed at that, then she went over and took Mayrose by the wrist. "Come on, Mama. We have better things to do than waste away on the backside of beyond with a pack of rednecks."

Mayrose knew when she'd lost a battle, and maybe even a war. She shook off Breanna's grip and flounced out, like she'd wanted to leave anyway.

Like it was *her* choice and anyway, they were all beneath her.

Kendall watched them go, surprised to find that she felt something like grief wash over her.

She loved that Belinda had left open the possibility for their return. And people could be surprising.

But, deep down, Kendall knew she wasn't going to see the Darlingtons again.

And that grief flowed through her. Not so much for losing her mother and her sister today. She'd never had them, not the way she'd wanted them.

This was more for the mother and sister she'd never had.

She stood there in the dining room of a pizza place that felt like home, that grief all over her, and watched them go. She watched the way the two of them swayed together as they walked, like two sides of the same too-shiny, counterfeit coin.

"You just don't like that she decided on her own to go," Breanna was saying, loud enough to float back inside. "We've talked about ditching her a million times. Let's take it as a win."

And she looked back over her shoulder to make sure that Kendall had heard that. To make sure that if there was any possibility of sinking in one last knife, she'd get it in there deep.

She and Kendall stared at each other for one last, long moment.

Breanna sneered. The door fell shut.

And for a moment, everybody inside Mountain Mama's was still.

Kendall felt that grief, yes, but beyond that, the heat of Harlan's hand on her neck. The comfort of the weight of his palm.

Belinda's tight grip on her hand.

The folks out on the patio remained frozen, in a hushed sort of silence. There was the sound of car doors slamming, an engine turning over, and then, at last, a car pulling away.

"I believe they're headed for Desolation Drive," the deputy sheriff said after a moment.

When he looked back inside, he exchanged a long look with Harlan. It made Kendall think that Mayrose and Breanna might have a tougher time out there then they imagined.

And she did not plan to do one tiny little thing about the

bed they'd made but let them sleep in it.

Belinda squeezed Kendall's hand in three short bursts, then let go. Harlan pulled her back into his chest, tipping her chin up so he could gaze down at her.

"Welcome to Cowboy Point, baby," he said, in that voice of his that carried, maybe all the way up to the peak of Copper Mountain, down into Marietta, and back. She couldn't imagine there was anywhere on this earth that couldn't hear Harlan Carey if he wanted them to. She hoped she'd never find out. "Welcome home."

And everybody cheered.

Chapter Twelve

AND FOR THE first time in her whole life, Kendall understood what it was to have a real family.

Not just a family, but *people*. A whole community.

They all streamed inside and somehow, what could have been just another rendition of the same old depressing Darlington family song turned into a party.

And then, quickly enough, it turned into a kind of wedding reception.

Because everyone came up to the two of them, Harlan and Kendall, to offer their congratulations. The Bennett sisters started bringing out food and drinks, someone picked up a guitar, and before Kendall knew it, she was laughing. And dancing.

And being twirled around the floor of the patio, there beneath that beautiful summer sky, by the men who had claimed her as a sister.

When they'd all had a turn, it was time for the man who'd called her his daughter.

"I never had a father, Zeke," she told him, only a little shyly.

"I never had a daughter, either," he retorted. "Said so."

"I think we'll make it work," Kendall said, and smiled so wide it made her cheeks hurt.

They danced a moment or two, and then he cleared his throat. "I think you're good for this family," Zeke told her gruffly. "And not only because you're going to sit in that booth tomorrow and convince tourists to buy my spurs."

"At exorbitant prices," Kendall agreed happily.

"I think you're good for him," Zeke said, nodding over at Harlan. "A man can get too used to being alone. He's better with you."

Kendall looked over at Harlan too, aware that she was flushed all over again. And Harlan was engaged in conversation with his friends, but he caught Kendall's eye. He always did. Because he always knew exactly where she was.

The kind of tracking device she could come to depend on, she thought, as his dark eyes gleamed, telling her he saw that flush too.

She couldn't wait to go home with him. To *their* home.

Kendall forced herself to return her attention to her father-in-law as he gently two-stepped them around. She studied him a moment, taking in his own flush, that looked a lot like good health to her. "Can I ask you something shocking?"

The old man looked at her, his gaze canny. "Careful you don't get too shocking. The old ticker isn't what it used to be."

"Are you really sick?"

Kendall regretted it the moment it left her mouth. Zeke frowned at her and she thought he was going to rescind all the nice things he'd said to her—

But then, still dancing, he grinned.

"Let's just say," he said, pulling her close and keeping his voice low, "that I wouldn't be surprised if the beautiful grandbabies you bring into this world one day trigger a remission."

She considered that. "A long remission?"

"You might very well give a man new life," Zeke replied, his eyes twinkling.

And then he sang along to the song as they kept on dancing.

When the song was done, he delivered her, at last, into the arms of her husband.

The husband she had never dreamed about, because she wouldn't have believed that he could be real. The husband who had changed everything, because *he* believed in *her*.

"I'm proud of you," Harlan told her now, pulling her into his arms and holding her while the music soared all around them. "I'm so damn proud of you, Kendall."

"It's because of you." She slid her hands up to his face and held them there, right where she wanted him. "I never could have stood up to them if you hadn't believed in me, Harlan. If you hadn't showed me the way."

"I didn't show you a thing," he said, smiling. "Except maybe who you've been all along, despite them."

"What I'm trying to say is that I love you," she told him, her gaze on his and her heart painful inside her chest. "I think it's possible I loved you from the very first moment I saw you, sitting in that booth in that saloon. I think—"

"You think?"

Kendall smiled, big and wide, and she didn't care if the whole world saw it. "I know. I love you, Harlan. It feels like I always have. I know I always will."

He gazed down at her, this good man who loved her back. Who looked at her and didn't see a Darlington. Who had made her a Carey. Who had given her a home.

Who was the first thing she wanted to see each morning and the last thing she wanted to see each night, and who she wanted to hold on to in between, curled up together like puzzle pieces that together made a beautiful whole.

"I know," he said, his mouth curving in the way she liked best. "Baby, I know. But I sure do like hearing it."

When he kissed her then, everybody cheered again. Louder this time.

And it was different, she understood. Their actual wedding had been like a handshake, a deal they'd made.

But this was a whole other kind of wedding. The *stand up in front of everyone who matters to you and promise you're going to love each other forever* kind of thing.

The *forever kind of thing* that was the very least of what they were going to be for each other.

Starting right here, right now.

So Kendall kissed him back. Then she smiled out at all these people who'd stood up for her. Her real family. Her true friends, and who cared if they were new. They'd get there.

She knew they would.

This was the whole fairy tale, right here, surrounded by pine and love and an endlessly blue Montana sky.

Her happy ever after was starting right now.

And with Harlan beside her, forever was a given.

Epilogue

"WELL, WELL, WELL," Belinda said happily the next morning, settling in with her coffee on the arm of Zeke's chair and raising her mug toward Alice, "I think this is going *splendidly*."

"Better than expected," Zeke agreed.

In her picture, captured forever young and bright, Alice seemed to smile straight at them, like she was giving her agreement.

"Though I think Kendall suspects," he felt compelled to say. When Belinda only looked at him, he shrugged. Only a little sheepishly. "I may have confirmed her suspicions, in fact."

"I like her." Belinda sighed contentedly. "She's perfect for Harlan and she's smart enough to see through you? That makes her the perfect daughter-in-law, and Lord knows, I need more women around here. She's an excellent start."

She was. There was no debating it.

But Zeke hadn't expected that he'd *want* the daughters-in-law his little gambit would bring him. Not *personally*. He hadn't given any thought to whether or not he would come to *like* them for themselves, having nothing to do with their relationships to his own children. How he would watch them with his sons and think of them as his own.

If Kendall was any indication of how this was going to go, he had four more women to meet and make room for in his gruff old heart.

There was a beautiful sort of discomfort in that. He really hadn't expected it.

A lot like he hadn't expected that telling his sons that he was dying would be… less entertaining and a whole lot more upsetting than he'd figured. He'd kind of glossed over the emotional part of all that in the planning stage, because *he* knew he was as healthy as a horse.

He'd been too busy focusing on the end goal. Grandchildren, yes, and his sons not so damned aloof and lonely all the time, no matter how many times they claimed they weren't.

A father knew.

Zeke hadn't been prepared for the way they'd all stared back at him that Easter Sunday after he'd made his announcement. Five grown men who'd looked, for a moment, like the toddlers they'd been so many years ago. All wide eyes and an unusual, heavy silence that had lasted too long.

He'd hated it.

Just like he hated the way they'd all treated him since, fluttering around him like a pack of hens. Extra careful. Extra solicitous, like he was visibly broken and might shatter at the first glance.

Like he was already gone.

Mind you, Zeke had been working this land his whole life. He knew how to hunker down and work with what he had for a season. Even if it was this nonsense.

Careful what you wish for had never rung more loudly in his own head.

Today, however, he settled back in his chair with Belinda on the arm and Alice at his elbow. Because today was a day for resting on laurels.

His laurels, thank you very much.

"One down," he said with great satisfaction. "Four to go."

"Hear, hear," Belinda said, clinking her mug to his, then to the edge of Alice's picture frame. "We got this. Grandbabies on tap."

Zeke gazed out at the beautiful view that never failed to lift his spirits and make his heart feel strong enough to rearrange all the mountains as he pleased. The endless blue sky and the trees that rose to meet it. The hills that soared above the tree line, many still with patches of snow. This glorious land that gave him so much. The first, great, endlessly enduring love of his life that had brought him all the rest of the things he loved.

And then he thought about the personalities of these boys he'd raised into men. The ways he knew them better than most and, in some ways, better than they knew themselves. A father's prerogative, he often thought. He'd held the whole of their lives in his hands so far and he would until he actually died, which he hoped was far off in the future.

Maybe, he thought now, it was time he did more than just issue a challenge and sit back.

Now that he knew the game was afoot, shouldn't he also take the opportunity to put a few things in motion?

The fact was, he should have known that Harlan would be the one to act quickly and decisively, to get the ball rolling. That was what Harlan did, each and every day. That was who Harlan was.

Zeke had started to wonder if they hadn't believed him before Kendall turned up. If he might have to make an even more dramatic announcement. Or play up that fragility they all seemed to think he was suddenly riddled with.

But now that he knew his plan was in action, Zeke figured he needed to make sure that things continued at the same pace.

Because a man could only take so much coddling from a pack of boys he'd diapered and burped, bandaged and rocked to sleep after nightmares, and taught to walk. And talk. And then, inevitably, talk back.

He held the marvel that was his Belinda close. He smiled at his sweet Alice in her frame.

And he allowed himself to think, deeply, about exactly how best he could rock each and every one of his sons' worlds. Maybe take them down a peg or two, problematic as they were to all the ladies in Cowboy Point—and beyond.

Starting with Wilder, Zeke thought, because the good Lord knew, the next oldest in line needed his world rocked a little bit. He was far too comfortable. Too arrogant, some might say.

But not for long.

Zeke would see to it. Personally.

He already knew how.

The End

More Books by Megan Crane

The Flint Brothers Take Montana series

Book 1: *Tempt Me, Cowboy*

Book 2: *Please Me, Cowboy*

Book 3: *Tempt Me Please, Cowboy*

The Greys of Montana Series

Book 1: *Come Home for Christmas, Cowboy*

Book 2: *In Bed with the Bachelor*

Book 3: *Project Virgin*

Book 4: *Most Dangerous Cowboy*

Book 5: *Have Yourself a Crazy Little Christmas*

Other titles

A Game of Brides

I Love the 80s

Once More with Feeling

Available now at your favorite online retailer!

About the Author

USA Today bestselling, multi-award-nominated, and critically-acclaimed author Megan Crane has written more than 145 books, and shows no sign of slowing down. She publishes romance as **Megan Crane** and **M.M. Crane** with an exciting backlist of women's fiction, rom-coms, chick lit, and young adult novels. She's also won a large and loyal fanbase as **Caitlin Crews** with Harlequin Presents, Harlequin Dare, Harlequin Historical, and contemporary cowboy books. And for paranormal fun, Megan partners with Nicole Helm to publish as **Hazel Beck** for her witchy rom-com novels.

Megan has a Masters and Ph.D. in English Literature, has taught creative writing classes in places like UCLA

Extension's prestigious Writers' Program, and is always available to give workshops (or her opinion). She lives in the Pacific Northwest with her comic book artist husband, though, at any given time, she is likely to either be huddled in a coffee shop somewhere or off traveling the world. Preferably both.

Thank you for reading

The Cowboy's Mail-Order Bride

If you enjoyed this book, you can find more from all our great authors at TulePublishing.com, or from your favorite online retailer.

TULE
PUBLISHING

Made in the USA
Las Vegas, NV
16 May 2024

89989735R00132